The Shadow Killers

They appeared out of the night, dark shadows on a deadly mission. Each of their victims suffered a violent and horrible death. Dorret Keene is sent to discover the perpetrator and the motivation behind the killings. But before he arrives at his destination, he kills a buffalo hunter.

Not only do the man's kin vow revenge, but also Keene is saddled with a child-bride and her unscrupulous drunkard of a husband. Finding the killers is like chasing a grain of sand in a dust storm. When the showdown finally comes, it will be a storm of gunfire and blood! Will Keene live to tell the tale?

The Shadow Killers

Terrell L. Bowers

A Black Horse Western

ROBERT HALE · LONDON

ISBN 0 7090 7318 6

Robert Hale Limited
Clerkenwell House
Clerkenwell Green
London EC1R 0HT

Typeset by
Derek Doyle & Associates, Liverpool.
Printed and bound in Great Britain by
Antony Rowe Limited, Wiltshire

CHAPTER ONE

Dorret Keene stood before the judge, head lowered respectfully, his hat in his hands. This was not the first time he'd been before the man.

'Mr Keene,' the judge spoke as if he was tired, 'how nice of you to pay us another visit.'

'It wasn't my fault, Your Honor,' he said quietly. 'Them Tarkington boys were making indecent remarks and there were ladies present.'

'It was the annual fair!' the judge growled. 'The Tarkington family is well thought of in the community. The two boys had been partying at the barbecue and drinking beer. I don't believe a couple harmless words constituted starting a brawl.'

Keene gave his head a shake. 'If a man stands by and lets anyone talk trash like that in front of female folks, them gals cease to be ladies. This here world won't be worth shucks once women cease being treated like ladies.'

'Now look here, Keene!' The judge was growing red in the face. 'You might think you're some kind of Don Quixote, but I assure you, I do not!'

'Don who?'

'A character in a book by a man named Cervantes,' the judge explained. 'He thought of himself as a gallant knight, one who would right the wrongs of the world single-handedly.'

'Sounds like the kind of man we need more of, Your Honor.'

The judge gave his head a violent shake. 'No! No! No!' he bellowed. 'I'm making a point, Keene! I'm not intending to offer up a role model for you!'

'Oh, sorry.'

'You're sorry?' the judge wailed. 'Every single time you come before me – I'm the one who is sorry! You're a hopeless troublemaker! You're too blasted good with both your gun and your fists! You are too quick to jump to defend the honor of a saloon-woman or beggar or thief! I ought to find you in contempt of court!'

Keene frowned. 'I don't have any contempt for the court, Your Honor. It's foul-mouthed drunks or men who don't mind their manners – them are the ones I have contempt for.'

The judge banged his gavel. 'That's it!' he shouted. 'I've had enough!'

But a large fellow, who had been sitting off in a corner and listening, stood up and lifted a hand to draw attention. The judge paused, before he suffered from apoplexy, to recognize the man.

'Yes? What is it?'

'The name is Konrad Ellington,' the man said. 'May I approach the bench, Your Honor?'

'Is this pertinent to the case before the court?'

'Yes, sir, it certainly is.'

The judge waved him forward and Keene waited as the man walked up to the desk. The two of them spoke in hushed tones for a minute, then a smile came on to the judge's face. He gave a nod and the large fellow returned to his seat.

'A proposal has been made to this court,' the judge announced. 'I am inclined to accept the terms and offer them to you, Dorrett Keene.'

Keene cast a quick glance over at the stranger. 'What terms, Your Honor?'

'You have a choice – thirty days in jail for disturbing the peace and testing the limits of my patience, or you can put on a badge and take on an assignment for the US marshal.' Another smile. 'Either way, you will be out of my hair for at least a month!'

'Me? A deputy?'

'Make up your mind, Keene. We haven't got all day.'

Keene gave a shrug of his shoulders, wondering what kind of mess he was getting himself into.

'Guess I'll pin on a badge, Your Honor.'

Keene was on the next train going west. At times, it passed through towns where buffalo-bones were stacked like cords of wood. The bleached bones formed small mountains, as they were stockpiled to await shipping back East to mills for manufacturing everything from fertilizer to bone china. On Keene's previous trip across the plains, the locomotive had often been forced to stop or slow down to plow through herds of wandering buffalo. On this journey, he saw only the decaying remains of a few slaughtered animals. The great herds of buffalo had been wiped from the face of the earth.

Other areas showed promise and progress. There were shipping pens being built along the railroad line. Soon, the cattle towns like Abilene would be rivaled by other stops all along the path of the railroad. There was even talk of going clear to El Paso with rail. As the Atchinson, Topeka and Santa Fe had already reached Santa Fe, New Mexico, that looked to be a foregone conclusion. The West was getting more crowded and shrinking in size almost daily. The buffalo were already gone, so were many of the Indian tribes. Next would be the herds of wild horses and the antelope.

Keene and his horse got off the train at Raton, New Mexico. He guessed it to be roughly a hundred miles to Buckshot from that jumping-off point. The trail would be over a range of mountains which separated the town from the plains and isolated it from Fort Union, the nearest army post. With Apache and Comanche still at war throughout New Mexico and Texas, a man traveled with his gun ready and didn't rely on help from the fort. The soldiers were spread too thin to do much about protecting a solitary rider. The hills were laced with Indian trails, so Keene hoped to make it to Buckshot in two days and in one piece – though not necessarily in that order!

He picked up a few needed supplies and got directions from a storekeeper. Buckshot, he learned, was nestled in a large basin, fed by plentiful streams and graced by an ample growing-season. It was perfect for raising cattle or farming. Except for one little drawback, it sounded like a perfect place to live. The Shadow Killers seemed intent on making it a perfect place to die!

Keene was still surprised that Konrad Ellington would ask him to look into a string of murders. As it turned out, Konrad was not even assigned to New Mexico Territory. He was usually involved with troubles further north. However, he was looking into the trouble because the US marshal's office had received a desperate request for help and there was no one available to check it out. It seemed several men had died and no one could identify the killers. Keene had no background as a detective, but he wasn't eager to spend a month in jail either. He would ride down to Buckshot, snoop around, and try to find out what was going on. If he failed, he would likely be replaced by an actual deputy marshal, as soon as one was free to look into the trouble.

Lyla Manning paused to wash her hair. The stream was cold, but she enjoyed the exhilaration of being clean. She didn't have a deep enough pool for swimming, but the water came up to her shoulders when she sat on the rocky bottom of the creek-bed.

Cecil was at the campsite, singing one of the disgusting tunes he had heard at some bar or saloon. She wished the man would either learn some decent songs or take up whistling. Every time he started drinking, he felt compelled to spout dirty lyrics.

Icy water ran down into her eyes as Lyla rinsed her hair. She rose up, waded to shore, and put a ragged towel to her face. After drying off as best she could, she donned her thin cotton dress and found a rock where she could sit in the sun. Warming herself from the cold bath, she began to brush the tangles out of her wet hair.

'We be too late, Joab,' a sleazy voice slurred, rudely interrupting her tranquillity. 'She done finished washing.'

Lyla sucked in her breath and leapt to her feet. She spied two scroungy men, partly hidden by the brush on the opposite bank. They wore dirty Kentucky jeans, cotton work-shirts and worn boots. Each had on a coonskin hat, which housed their long, greasy-looking black hair. One man had a thick mustache, while the other had several days' growth of beard on his face. They both stared hard at her, their eyes traversing over her body like dirty fingers, probing, touching, violating her.

The one with the mustache spoke up. 'Maybe she'll get dirty again fer us, Seth. I'd sure fancy a look at her bare neked.'

Both men laughed coarsely and Lyla beat a hasty retreat. She darted through the brush and ran to the camp site. Cecil had stopped singing. He was confronted by two more of the same breed of men. One was fairly young, in his early twenties, while the other man had streaks of gray in both his hair and his short, pointed beard. He was obviously the elder statesman of the group. Lyla kept moving, until she could stand a few feet behind Cecil.

'Light down and share the fire!' Cecil greeted the strangers. 'Kin I offer you fellers a drink?'

'How about it, pa?' the young one asked the grizzled old man.

'Hush, Zeke,' the elderly man said.

These two were dressed like the pair who had discovered Lyla sunning herself. The smell of dried blood emanated from both of them. There were stains on their boots and jeans which gave evidence of their bloody profession.

'Buffalo hunters, ain't you?' Cecil reached the same conclusion about their occupation. However, he was too drunk to be wary of any danger.

'That's right, you old sot.' Zeke laughed. 'Are you offering to share just the jug, or do the little filly thar go with the hospitality?'

Cecil chuckled inanely. 'My name's Cecil Clemons,' he introduced himself. 'The gal here is my wife.'

The news put a curious look on Zeke's face. 'Looks a mite young for you, Clemons,' he said. 'You steal her out of the cradle?'

Cecil uttered another silly laugh. 'Traded for her – a couple mules and thirty dollars. I needed someone to bend and serve to my needs.'

'What about it, Pa?' the boy said. 'We gonna have us a drink?'

The man gave his shaggy head an affirmative nod. 'Mayhaps we will join you fer a snort or three, Clemons,' he said, as the two boys from the stream arrived to stand alongside the old man. 'This here be my family.' He motioned around at each of the boys and introduced them. 'Joab, Seth and Zeke.' He thumped himself on the chest, 'and I be Isaac Hayden.'

'Glad to know all of you.' Cecil was cordial. 'We made our camp here to take advantage of the stream. The wife caught up a mess of natives for supper. We've more fish than we kin eat. You're welcome to join us.'

Lyla saw two of the boys exchange derisive grins. The third one continued to leer openly at her, as if

11

Cecil had listed her on the evening menu.

'We can stay fer a pass of the jug,' Isaac said, 'but we need to get going in time to make Raton this evening. I've some business thar.'

'Sure, sure,' Cecil replied. 'I know how it is.'

The four men tied off their horses, then came over to the fire. The jug made a couple of passes, while Lyla busied herself with making beds for the night. The dirty man with the mustache came over to watch her. She recalled him being the one called Joab.

'I like watching a woman move about,' he slurred through a mouthful of tobacco. He paused to spit, then let his eyes roam freely over her. ' 'Specially, a fine-looking woman.'

She attempted to ignore him.

'So you're married to that old drunk, huh?' Joab asked, getting a bit closer to her.

Lyla carefully stepped over the blankets to keep out of the man's reach. She didn't meet his vulgar eyes, wishing the whole disgusting bunch would hurry the friendly drink and then get on their way.

Joab appraised her candidly. 'Bet a coot like him don't stir your blood none.'

Lyla experienced a flush of embarrassment. She flicked another nervous glance over at Cecil. Why didn't he pay any mind to what was going on? Didn't he realize these men were nothing but trouble? Did his drinking make him completely blind?

Joab picked up a short, broken, tree-branch. As Lyla turned to get the fixings for the string of fish, he used the end of the stick to lift the corner of her dress.

Lyla had taken hold of a frying-pan. When she felt the dress being raised up above her knees, she swung the skillet about in a panic!

Joab had ducked his head, in order to get a better look at her legs. The awkward position cost him any chance to react to her wielding of the pan. She bonked him right on the skull!

'Ye-ow!' Joab cried out, holding both hands over his battered head.

'What in thunder is going on?' Isaac bellowed. 'What's that wife of yourn done to my boy?'

Cecil staggered across the clearing and put accusing eyes on Lyla. His red-rimmed eyes clouded with an immediate anger. 'What's the idea, woman?' he demanded to know. 'Why did you hit the boy?'

'He tried to lift up my dress!' she explained hastily.

Cecil chuckled. 'Looks like your boy got a little careless with his peeking, Isaac. My wife is a might testy about being looked at or touched.'

Isaac didn't see the humor of the situation. He was busy examining the bump on Joab's forehead. The pan had split the skin enough to make the injury bleed. There wasn't much actual damage, but the trickle of blood made the wound look more serious.

'She done cracked open my boy's skull!' Isaac bellowed. 'I ain't going to stand fer that sort of thing, Clemons!'

'Ah, it ain't bad.' Cecil tried to soothe his ire. 'It didn't even knock the boy silly.'

But Isaac nodded to his two other sons. They quickly took hold of Cecil and began to bind him with a short length of rope.

'Whoa! Hold on there,' Cecil blubbered. 'I didn't do nothing!'

Isaac took a step toward Lyla and made a grab for her.

She still held the skillet. She flung it at him to ward him off. He was quick enough to block the pan from hitting anything but his hands and forearm. Even so, it gave Lyla the opportunity to scamper off into the nearby woods.

'I'll handle the drunk!' Isaac roared to his sons. 'Go fetch that she-cat back here!'

Lyla didn't look over her shoulder. She splashed through the stream of water, running hard. Then she was dodging trees and scrambling up between the rocks and tangled brush. Terror put speed into her legs and she was as sure-footed as a deer.

'Ye-hah, Zeke!' one of the Hayden boys yelled. 'Thar she goes! She's heading fer the main trail!'

'Get ahead of her, Seth!' Zeke called back. 'Cut her off!'

Lyla climbed at a run, her heart thundering within her chest, her lips parted to draw in more air. Frantic to get away, she kept her legs pumping. She had to escape!

Keene pulled his horse to a stop and put his hand on his gun. He saw a fleeting shadow cross the trail ahead on the dead run. Even as he thought of the Kiowa or Apache and a possible attack, he saw two ragged looking hunters come into view.

Uncertain as to what was happening, Keene swung his mount behind a thicket of buckbrush. He dismounted and slipped quietly up the side of the mountain, attempting to get in front of the action. He would have a look, but he didn't want any trouble.

However, his luck took a downward turn – the same as the fleet-footed prey. Before he could react and get out of the way, a wet, puffing, wild-eyed female ran headlong into him! He grunted from the impact and the two of them went down in a tangle of arm and legs.

'What the. . . ?' he tried to speak.

The young woman began to flail away at him with balled fists, until she caught sight of Keene's face. Then, instead of fighting him, she threw herself into his arms and clung to him.

'Help me!' she murmured softly, whimpering fearfully. 'Please help me!'

Keene attempted to get back up on to his feet, but the girl would not release her hold around his neck.

'Easy there, little lady,' he spoke softly to her, while keeping watch for the two men chasing after her. 'No one is going to hurt you.'

'Yo, Seth!' a voice called out from a short way off. 'She done back-tracked us again'!'

'Which way?' the other hollered back.

Eventually able to remove the girl's arms from his neck, Keene rose to a standing position. He slipped the thong off his gun as he heard the two men approach through the trees. The young woman slipped around behind him, still clinging tightly to his left arm and quivering with fright.

Two dirty, long-haired, buffalo hunters appeared on the trail. Keene guessed they were probably in their mid-twenties and each was wearing a gun and a knife. Neither had a weapon drawn, as they hadn't expected to find Keene in their path. They stopped and stared at him as if he was some kind of spook.

'Howdy, boys,' Keene greeted the two men. 'You wouldn't mind telling me why you're chasing the young lady here, would you?' He kept his voice friendly, while resting his hand on the butt of his short-barrel Peacemaker .45.

The two exchanged looks, then one stepped forward. He appeared to be the older of the pair.

'What fer do you want to mix into this, stranger?'

'I asked you a question first,' Keene replied curtly. 'What's the meaning of scaring this gal half to death?'

The other shrugged. 'She done clubbed brother Joab with a skillet. Pa thought she ought tuh get a whupping fer that.'

Keene stood poised against the two men. Both had the leather thong over the hammer of their Navy Colts. If it came to a fight, they would be extremely slow to get their guns into play. However, he didn't wish for the predicament to escalate into a dual killing.

'Maybe we ought to go see your pa,' he offered. 'I'd as soon avoid any trouble.'

'You kin avoid trouble by handing over that little viper.'

'I don't think so,' Keene said, adding a cool tint to his words. 'And you boys don't want to force the issue . . . else I'll likely have to kill you both.'

'Sure fancies himself, don't he, Seth?' one asked the other.

'He sure 'nuff do, Zeke,' the second replied. 'But Pa wouldn't like us killing no one without him giving the say-so.'

'Yonder is the camp,' the one called Seth nodded.

'You boys lead the way,' Keene said. 'The lady and I will be right behind you.'

After a moment's hesitation, the two ragged men turned around and started threading their way through the brush.

Keene picked up his horse and got astride. He pulled the girl up behind him and they kept pace with the two hunters. The girl was like a second shadow, with both hands fastened around his middle. He mentally cussed himself for allowing the shaggy men to keep their guns. He could have handled the two of them, but they were going to join their pa and another brother. How many men was he going up against?

It was a little late to worry. Unless he turned his horse the other way and rode for Buckshot, he was committed. He didn't want any hostile men on his back-trail, so he would talk to the old man. Maybe he would listen to reason.

The camp had been readied for the night, with a pair of beds laid out and a coffee-pot near a crackling fire. Next to the circle of rocks for the fire-pit was an old gent, lying on his side, bound up like a calf ready for branding. Standing over him was another buffalo hunter. He didn't look like the friendly sort.

'Who you brung back with you?' the man asked the two boys.

'The name is Dorret Keene,' Keene spoke up. 'Who are you?'

'We be the Hadens,' the old man answered. 'I be Isaac, and them be my boys.'

'I met your offspring while they were chasing after

17

this young woman.' Keene spoke matter-of-factly, watching the three men together. He wondered what had happened to the fourth man. The two strays had claimed the girl had hit their brother.

So where is he?

Isaac glared past Keene at the girl, then narrowed his gaze. 'You don't want to be butting into this, Keene. We've a mind to teach the wildcat a lesson.'

Keene's eyes swept the camp rapidly. The man on the ground had a dirty rag betwixt his teeth, but he gave a sharp nod of his head to show the right direction. Keene looked that way – just in time to see the injured hunter taking aim at him!

Rolling out of the saddle, he knocked the young woman over the back of the horse. The blast of a gun filled the air, but the bullet sailed harmlessly past Keene's chin and impacted into a nearby tree.

Keene's horse danced out of the way as he brought his own gun to bear. Before the hunter could fire again, Keene's gun bucked in his hand, spitting fire and lead. He placed two slugs into the hunter's chest and spun around to cover the other three.

Isaac held his hand in front of the other two boys, stopping them from trying to draw their guns. His teeth were anchored, eyes set, as he waited for the smoke to clear. Then he strode over and looked at his son's body.

'You kilt my boy, Keene!' he thundered, after a short examination. 'By all the demons in hell, I'll see you dead fer this!'

'When you draw a bead on a man from ambush,' Keene replied, 'getting killed is always a possibility.' Then, keeping his gun on the three of them, he ordered them to drop their weapons into a pile and release the man at the fire.

Keene learned that the bound-up man was Cecil Clemons and got the story of how Joab had gotten a bump on his head from the girl. He supervised the burying of Joab Hayden by his kin, then took the men's horses and guns. To leave them stranded and unarmed, with hostile Indians around, might have been a death sentence. Even though the temptation was great to let them take their chances, Keene had too much of a conscience for that. He tied the three men to a tree, knowing they would work themselves loose in several hours.

'I'll leave your horses up the trail four or five miles to the west. Once you pick them up, I'd advise you to forget coming after me. I've no stomach for killing any more of you buffalo hunters.'

'You kin quit crying, Keene,' Isaac sneered. 'Me and my boys will track you to the ends of the earth. One shot is all we'll need to end your days. You kin mark my words, Keene. I'm aiming to see a grave with your name on it!'

'Ought to finish them right now,' Cecil told Keene, having broken camp and packed their gear back on his own two horses. 'They tied me up and was going to give Lyla a beating. They is nothing but scum, Keene, pure scum.'

'I can't execute them for making threats against me, Clemons.'

'They'll come after you,' the drunk responded. 'Ought to settle it here and now.'

Keene didn't reply, but he knew Cecil was right. He

wished there was some way to end it there and then, but he wasn't the kind of man to kill in cold blood. He mounted up and started toward the main trail. He led the four Hayden horses, while Cecil and the girl stuck alongside. It was still a long trek to Buckshot, and it would be dark soon. However, the sky was clear and there would be a full moon. It would be difficult, but not impossible to ride on through for most of the night.

'Your daughter don't talk much,' said Keene to the old man.

Cecil had been taking a pull on his jug. He cast a glance over at the girl and shook his head. 'She ain't my daughter, Keene . . . she's my wife. I married her a few months back. She does chores and cooks to earn her keep.'

Keene glanced at the girl, but she avoided meeting his stare. Her expression wasn't distinguishable in the dusk, but he thought she was blushing from shame.

'What brings you into the wilds of New Mexico Territory, Keene?' Cecil asked.

'Trouble,' he answered. 'And I just doubled my chances of getting killed.'

'Them hunters won't quit. The old man was bragging about what they were going to do to Lyla. I'm telling you, Keene, you ain't seen the last of those mad dogs.'

Keene figured Cecil was stating the obvious. He would have to keep a sharp watch for the buffalo hunters. With their skill with a high-power rifle, they only had to get within a quarter-mile to be in range. That wasn't a pleasant thought.

Keene considered Lyla for a moment. Why would a

young woman marry a man like Cecil? Besides being a drunk, he seemed to be one of the shiftless, wandering bums in the West. He was certainly not the kind of man to have been her first choice of companion.

Even as he considered her plight, she lifted her eyes enough to look at him with a coy glance. She shifted her gaze at once and he smiled inwardly. She was a pretty girl, even with wind-blown hair, dressed in rags and tear-streaks on her cheeks. He wondered how she would look with a touch of rouge and in a proper dress.

Keep your mind on business! he told himself. He had to deal with a pack of killers, who were terrorizing Buckshot. He was supposed to discover the who and why behind those raids. As he rode, he considered the list of dead men: Cowans, who had been the sheriff, was found hanging from a tree; a farmer named Jones was drowned in a creek; Billings, who co-shared ownership of the bank was dragged to death behind a horse; and Joe Layton, a rancher, was killed by a stampede. Each had been left with a note on their chest. The words: 'it's your time to die!' were printed in bold letters on the page. The murders bespoke of revenge or a vendetta of some kind, but Konrad said they didn't have a clue as to the motive behind the killings. It would take both skill and luck for him to discover the truth about the Shadow Killers.

While seeking answers, he also had to keep an eye out for Isaac Hayden and his two remaining moron sons. He cast a swift glance at the young lady and sighed inwardly. He wasn't going to have time to be day-dreaming about a pretty girl . . . especially one who was already married!

CHAPTER TWO

Buckshot was a fair-sized settlement. Surrounded by several ranches, there were also a number of farms at the lower end of the basin, while mining operations were active in the nearby mountains. The town was off the beaten track for trail drives, but the gold- and silver-mines needed supplies and shipped their freight out of Buckshot for Santa Fe. That brought in enough money to keep the little burg thriving.

Keene was surprised to see a dozen stores and a couple big casinos in town. The jail looked fairly new, but there was a sign on the door which said SHERIFF WANTED. He reined his horse up in front of the first two-story structure he came to. It was also freshly whitewashed and boasted a sign offering rooms, meals and baths.

'This looks like a good place to rest up,' he told Clemons.

The old man grunted sourly, 'It belongs to Fred Smith. He don't give credit.'

'You know him, do you?'

'Yeah.' Clemons slurred the words distastefully. 'He's the town mayor.'

'Well, where do you usually hang your hat in this town?'

'I usually get into the loft at the livery. The hostler there only charges a few cents for me and my horses. I don't waste good money putting a fancy roof over my head.'

'And your wife?'

'She stays wherever I stay,' Cecil answered, with a wave of his hand. 'She's used to making do, same as me.'

Keene flicked a glance at the girl. She didn't meet his look, hiding her mortification behind lash-adorned lids and a lowered head. It grated against his conscience that the young woman was treated with such a lack of common decency.

'If it's all the same to you, Clemons, I'm going to get two rooms – one for myself and one for the lady. You can do whatever you want.'

He might have expected the old gent to object, but he did just the opposite. His eyes filled with an instant enthusiasm.

'You want to hire out my missus?' his voice was eager. 'You need someone to clean for you, curry your horse, treat your saddle or boots with polish or oil?'

'I only offered to get her a room. I'm not looking to hire a servant.'

'That's what she's good at, Keene. She does about any kind of work there is.' He gave a disgusting wink. 'Just don't expect no personal favors.'

'Clemons . . .'

'I'll rent her into your service, real inexpensive too,' Clemens hurried on. 'You can name the price – I figure you to be a fair man.'

Lyla's lips were pressed into a tight line. Her chin was tucked low enough, it nearly rested at the junction of her collar bones. She was obviously humiliated at the way Cecil tried to push her off on a total stranger.

'You do what you want,' Keene repeated to Clemons harshly. 'Like I said, I'll see the lady has a room for tonight.'

'Good, good!' the old souse said with a chuckle. 'Yes, sir, that'll be just dandy. I'll check around and see if I can get some work at one of the local taverns. Maybe I can earn some eating-money.'

Keene regarded the man with open contempt. He didn't doubt that Clemons's main interest was in getting himself another bottle of red-eye. He had deserted his poor, unfortunate, wife for a man he didn't even know.

Keene dismounted, as Clemons headed up the street. He draped the reins of his horse over a hitching pole and went around to the girl. A number of people were staring in their direction. Lyla was forced to ride astride and her flimsy dress revealed her legs up to her knees. To expose so much flesh was not only unladylike, it was indecent.

He first tied off her animal and then stretched up his arms for the girl. Lyla wasn't used to being treated like a member of the fairer sex. She hesitated at the gentlemanly gesture to help her down, then practically fell into his waiting arms. It was all he could do to save her a degree of modesty, lifting her down to the ground next to him. He quickly led the way into the hotel.

The man behind the counter had been working over a set of account-books. He put down the pen and lifted his head to greet the potential customers. Upon seeing the young woman, he bared his teeth and scowled at her.

'You ain't bringing that dirty thief in here, mister! Last time she and that old drunk took a room, they stole everything that wasn't tied down!'

Keene tightened his grip on Lyla, as she drew back, ready to bolt from the room.

'The young lady is my guest,' he told the man evenly. 'If anything turns up missing from her room, I'll stand good for it.'

But the man marched round and haughtily blocked their path. He was about the same size as Keene, but he was soft from working with a pencil and broom. His chest had sunk into the basement to form a roll of table muscle about his middle.

'You take your little piece of white trash to the barn, mister.' He pointed down the street with a stubby finger. 'Put her in a pen with the other animals . . . where she belongs!'

Keene didn't reply . . . in words. His rock-hard set of knuckles exploded against the clerk's jaw. It came without any warning, preventing the man from escaping the velocity behind the punch.

The blow sent him back-pedaling into the counter. He hit the wooden front and slowly slid down to a sitting position. His eyes were wide and glazed, his mouth agape and arms slack at his sides. Groggily, his head rolled on his shoulders.

'What's going on here!' a new, indignant voice demanded.

Keene turned to meet a scrawny, white-haired gent. He wore a suit and tie, with a fancy new derby hat in his hands. The man's look went from the clerk on the floor, quickly to the ragged Lyla, then rested on Keene. 'What's the meaning of this?'

'The oaf on the floor there was sorely lacking in common courtesy,' Keene said sharply. 'I was pointing out his lack of upbringing.'

The man hurried over to stand above the clerk. As that dazed individual seemed to regain his senses, the old boy gave him a hand in getting to his feet.

'You all right, Jake?' he asked the stunned clerk.

The man was unsteady, but rubbed his jaw and glared at Keene. 'I told him he couldn't bring the girl in here,' he said. 'The last time she and that bum, Clemons . . .'

The white-haired gent held up a hand to forestall any further explanation. Then he whirled about to face Keen.

'What are you doing with Clemons's concubine? She . . .'

Keene's hand flashed out and he caught hold of the man's shirt. Before he could finish his sentence, Keene yanked him forward so hard, he about came out of his shoes. Angrily, Keene thrust his jaw to within a few inches of the guy's face.

'It appears to me that there are a lot of ignorant

slobs in Buckshot. You could use a lesson or two in manners too.'

The man threw up his hands in a defensive gesture, losing his hat in the process. His complexion blanched and fear leapt into his eyes. He shook his head violently back and forth.

'Wait a minute, stranger! I don't want no trouble!'

Keene twisted the material tighter. 'Calling the young lady names in my presence is asking to get wooden teeth. You can either apologize or make an appointment with the local dentist!'

'Wait!' the man cried fearfully. 'I apologize! For heaven's sake! I'm sorry!'

'Yeah,' the clerk joined in, less than eager to incur any more of Keene's wrath. 'He's real sorry.'

Keene might have continued his assault, but a restraining hand from Lyla touched his arm. He glanced back at her and saw her eyes were glistening with tears. She gave a slight shake of her head and it instilled in him an immediate calm.

'Look here, *gentlemen*,' he explained patiently, releasing his grip on the man's shirt, 'all I want is a couple rooms. I'll stand good for anything that turns up missing.'

'By all means!' the old man replied, suddenly eager to please. 'Whatever you like.'

'About the baths. . . .'

'At once!' he agreed instantly. 'We have a boiler in the back. Jake will bring up one of our portable tubs to each of your rooms within the half-hour. Whatever you and the young lady need – you only have to ask.'

27

Keene swallowed his wrath and followed the clerk around the counter with his eyes. The man opened a ledger and turned it to a blank page.

'Your name, please?' the clerk asked professionally.

'Dorret Keene.'

That brought an exclamation from the man in the suit. 'K-Keene!' he sputtered. 'From the US marshal's office?' He was incredulous. 'I'm the one who sent for you!'

Keene heaved a sigh. Konrad would be real proud of the first impression his special deputy had made on the citizenry asking for help. Yep, real proud.

Lyla locked the door and put a chair under the latch, eager to succumb to the enticement of the tub of hot water. She pulled the curtain closed on the solitary window, slipped out of her dirty clothes, then tested the temperature of the bath. It was hot enough to send up tendrils of steam. She disturbed their upward ascent by drawing a path in the water with her fingers. She added a few drops of sweet-smelling oil, which had been provided by the clerk. There was also soap, a sponge for washing and a bath towel. Here was a luxury she had never before experienced . . . an actual bath in a bathing-tub.

She stepped over the side and gingerly settled into the hot water. The warmth penetrated her every pore as she sank down slowly. As she leaned back and rested her head against the side, the water rose to a level a few inches below her chin. She uttered a sigh of pleasue and relaxed completely.

It was a sensual delight, to soak in scented water, to

allow the heat to relieve the stress and soreness in her tired, aching muscles. She playfully lifted the washing-sponge over her head and squeezed. It sent a trickle of water on to her hair and down into her face. She was unable to stifle a giggle at the way a trail of soapy suds found their way to the end of her nose. She stirred up a handful of soap suds and lifted them in the palm of her hand. With a puff, she sent an array of bubbles floating off into the air.

After a few minutes of fun, she reclined once more, with her head against the wall of the tub. A slender smile of contentment played along her lips. When had she been this happy? It had been such a long time.

Her horrid present situation sought to invade her consciousness, but she dismissed the bad feelings at once. She was not going to let anything ruin the moment.

Seeking to think of something pleasant, she pictured Keene in her mind's eye. His image adequately suppressed the abominable visions of Cecil. He was like a story-book hero, a tower of strength, a gentleman. He was unlike any man she had ever met.

It seemed a lifetime ago, when her father had bartered her, his eldest daughter, to save the rest of the family from starvation. It had been the last time she'd seen her mother, three younger brothers and two younger sisters.

Keene was quite different from Cecil. He was a take-charge type of man. He wasn't the sort to stand by and let anyone insult her, whether she had it coming or not. As proof, the hotel clerk was going to be sporting a shiner. Keene could not have doubted that she and Cecil had stolen from the hotel. In fact, Cecil had taken the towels, bedding, the pitcher and wash-pan – even the pillow from their room. He had traded most of the items for a bottle of whiskey. The towel was a gift to Lyla, the only one she had to her name. The clerk had been within his rights to be indignant and resentful about allowing her back into one of their rooms. However, Keene had set him straight at once – Fred Smith too. She was *his* guest, and as such, she was to be treated with the utmost respect.

His image was clear in her mind. Better than average-looking, with dark hair and eyes, a slender, almost wiry build and there was a masculine manner in his movements and walk. He had a confidence about him – not conceit or arrogance, but rather a total lack of self-doubt. He obviously wasn't a man to back away from trouble, as proven by his defending her honor twice. His actions spoke of his character, for he likely believed Lyla had no honor to defend.

'Ma'am?' a voice shattered her intimate thoughts. She started, sitting up so quickly that a portion of water splashed over the side of the tub.

'Yes?' she replied timidly.

'When you're done with the bath, I've left a package at your door. I don't mean to toss my loop at another man's horse, but it's something I'd like for you to have.'

'All right,' she murmured, wondering what he was talking about.

'Be seeing you,' he added, as he went away.

She didn't speak in return, uncertain as to how she

should respond. It was difficult to know how to behave. She legally belonged to Cecil. She had no life or say of her own.

Keene walked down the hallway and went into the lobby. The mayor and two other men were waiting for him. As Keene joined them, the mayor led the way into a side-office, which was located behind the counter in the lobby. Inside the room were enough chairs for all of them.

The mayor sat behind a large oak desk. The others each took a wooden chair, with Keene in the middle.

Smith took charge of the meeting. 'To your right is Todd Billings.' He introduced a young man in a suit. 'He's now the sole owner of the bank. His brother was one of the men killed by these notorious killers.' He nodded to the other man. He was along in years and weather-beaten from long hours under the sun. 'The gent on your left is Ben Carter. He owns a farm at the edge of town. He's a member of the town council.'

'Proud to know you,' Keene said cordially. 'I'm Dorret Keene, a special deputy sent here by the US marshal.'

'We're getting desperate,' Ben spoke up. 'First Cowans, then Jones and Billings. Now Joe Layton is dead. It seems as if these raiders want to wipe out the entire valley.'

Keene leaned forward in his chair and studied each man. Fear was imbedded in the depths of their eyes. These were not cowardly men who could be easily frightened. With the exception of young Billings, Smith and Carter had probably fought for either the

North or South during the war. With the settlement of Buckshot being located in Indian country, they had probably also done their share of battling war parties over the past dozen years. They wouldn't have wired for help unless they were desperate.

'We need to concentrate first on the men who have been killed,' said Keene. 'We need to learn the motive behind these murders. Are these killers attacking people at random, or is there an ulterior purpose behind the murders. It's important that you share whatever information you have with me.'

'We intend to co-operate fully, Keene,' Smith assured him. 'For all we know, any one of us might be the next victim.'

'All right then. I need a complete history of this town and the men living here. I want to know what the dead men have in common – any mutual ties, past actions or whatever. I'll also want to see a copy of every edition of your town newspaper.'

Smith took out a piece of paper and began to jot down the men's names. Then the group listed every-thing they could think of under the different names. It was a lengthy summary of each man and what contributions he'd made to the town. From the personal history, they turned to common events that each man had taken part in.

Keene spent two solid hours with the three men. Then he collected the pages of notes Smith had scrib-bled for him. Among the papers were a list of names – close friends and relatives of each victim. The job ahead would require more than simple footwork. He had to discover the reason behind the killings, before he could start an actual search for the murderers.

He went up to his rented room, intending to study the notes in private. However, Lyla was waiting for him. She had been sitting patiently on the edge of his bed. As he entered, she immediately got to her feet.

Keene had to stop and stare at her. Even with her raven hair still damp, it flowed evenly down on to her shoulders like shinning threads of black velvet. The plain cotton dress he'd purchased for her was a butter-yellow in color, with white lace at the shoulders and collar. It couldn't have set off her deep mahogany eyes better if it had been designed especially for her.

'Ma'am ... Mrs Clemons ...' he struggled to gather his wits.

Lyla didn't look directly at him, but stood with her hands clasped self-consciously in front of her. A pink hue put added color in her cheeks, as she allowed him a candid inspection.

'You shouldn't have bought me a dress,' she murmured. 'I'm not your responsibility.'

'Seeing you in the dress is payment enough for me,' Keene replied. 'I hope it doesn't make your husband angry.'

'Cecil bought me, Mr Keene. I'm not his wife ... I'm his property.'

'Did a preacher say the words?' he asked.

The girl responded by lowering her head. 'Yes. It was the only way he would give my father the two mules and the money.'

There was a ache in Keene's chest, as if his heart was encased in broken glass. He was sympathetic for the girl, but there was nothing he could do. 'It is a real down-to-earth shame, ma'am,' he said gently. 'It really is.'

Lyla's eyes were misted over, but she managed a pleasant smile. 'It's a very pretty dress, Mr Keene. Thank you so very much.'

'My pleasure, ma'am,' he replied. 'Like I said, it's well worth the price just to see you wearing it.'

Lyla gave him a second short smile and hurried from his room. He wondered again if Cecil might get the wrong idea. A stranger wasn't supposed to pay for a bath and room for a man's wife, then give her a dress too. If places were reversed, he'd have gone after Cecil with a gun or club!

Keene pondered over the papers he'd gathered. He had the Buckshot's history from two different sources and a chronicle from the town sign painter, who also put out a monthly newsletter. He had come to Buckshot with some of the first settlers. His news-worthy tidbits included everything from recipes and new babies to accounts of fights, feuds and the few court trials held in Buckshot. The stack of newslet-ters was a big one, for it covered fifteen years of events.

Keene sorted information into groups, from each man's personal history to their known relatives. He tried to pinpoint anything which associated the four victims. He was sure there had to be a link between them, something which added up to a motive for these murders.

He finally decided to go see Smith. It was possible

a couple of the victims had diaries or kept a journal of some kind. There might be something written down that would help.

Once downstairs, Jake informed Keene that Smith was over at a nearby casino. Keene thanked him and went outside. He had taken a few steps up the street, when he noticed a disturbance down at the livery end of town. It was too dark to see clearly, but it appeared as if two men on horses were chasing after another man, who was on foot.

Grabbing up the nearest horse, Keene jerked the reins free and swung aboard. Then he sent the animal up the street at a run. It could have been the shadows, but it looked as if the riders had masks or hoods over their faces!

'Hold it!' Keene shouted, racing up the street.

The man on foot spied him coming and skidded to a stop. He was panic-stricken and suddenly reversed his direction. In his confusion, he ran away from Keene – right back into the other two riders!

Even as Keene bore down on them, one of the two hooded figures emptied the contents from a bucket on to the running man. He covered his eyes and stumbled to his knees. Keene, from a hundred yards away, was frozen in a moment of space and time, when he saw the second rider had a torch!

Keene made a grab for his gun, but he was too slow and too far away. The shadowy rider used the fiery club to strike his prey. Flames erupted in the night and the man was instantly engulfed in a suit of fire! He screamed in terror, waving his arms about wildly. He staggered up on to his feet, trying in vain to run away from the flames.

Keene yanked his horse to a bone jarring halt, searching for a target. But the specter-like shadows were gone, vanished into the blackness of the night. He holstered his pistol and jumped down. He fumbled to loosen the bedroll from behind the saddle, seeking to grab something with which he could beat out the fire.

The burning man fell on to his face, the flames having devoured both clothing and flesh from his entire body. Keene raced to his side and used the blanket to extinguish the fire. The Shadow Killers had struck again . . . this time, with his help!

Todd Billings and a young woman hurried over to his side, along with several other people who had been drawn out by the commotion. Keene finished snuffing out the last of the flames, but he knew it was too late. The air was filled with lingering smoke and the smell of burnt flesh. It took only a glance at the victim's charcoal condition to know he was dead. Keene carefully covered the man with the blanket he'd taken from the borrowed horse.

'Who is it?' Todd was the first to speak.

'I don't know,' Keene replied. 'I spotted him up the street, running from a couple riders. I grabbed a horse and tried to come to his aid, but he thought I was with the killers. He turned and ran away from me . . . right back into their laps.'

Smith had heard his words, having come rushing to join them. He looked down at the body and gasped to catch his breath.

'Big help you are, Keene,' he panted between

words. 'You show up just in time to help the Shadow Killers get another victim.'

'Look at his boots!' the young woman pointed to the dead man's feet. 'Those buckles. . . .' She sucked in her breath and fainted right into Todd's arms.

'It's the blacksmith!' Smith exclaimed. 'He always wore flat-heeled work boots with silver-dollar buckles. It's Hack Shawn.'

A couple men viewed the corpse and concurred with his assumption. The dead man was the town blacksmith. To all who knew him, he didn't have an enemy in the world.

'Did any of you see anything?' Keene asked the group, looking anxiously at the sea of faces. 'Anyone get a look at the raiders?'

'We heard his death screams,' Todd explained, cradling the girl in his arms. 'I was taking Tish home. She had joined me and my mother for dinner. We were on our way to pick up the carriage, over at the livery.'

Another of the men spoke up. 'I didn't hear nothing till Hack's horrid cries in the night.'

'There was too much noise in the casino,' added another spectator.

It was the same for all of them, except for one sandy-haired young man. When Keene looked at him, he grinned.

'All I seen was some guy grabbing my horse. I thought he was stealing him, so I run out to the street. Turns out you're what? Some kind of lawman?'

Keene tipped his head toward the horse he'd borrowed. 'Yours?'

'Yep. I was about to get myself something to eat.'

'Sorry I didn't have time to ask permission, friend. Glad you didn't come out shooting.'

'No need to explain,' he said, with a dismissive wave of his hand. 'Too bad you didn't do some good.'

Keene grunted. 'About the opposite, I'm afraid. The blacksmith ran from me. I helped to drive him back to his very death.'

'I did see that much,' the man said. 'Looked like there were two riders up the street. One had a bucket or something and the other had a torch. They got to the blacksmith before you could get there to help.'

'You got a name, fellow?'

'J.T. Reynolds,' he answered easily. 'I work at the Little Star Mine. It ain't much, but we scratch out enough to get by.'

'What now, Keene?' Smith was questioning him again. 'Do we form a posse or are we going to sit here?'

'Can't find anything out there in the dark. Come first light, I'll see if I can pick up any sign. I doubt I'll have much luck, but it's worth a look-see.'

'There's a tracker in town,' a man offered. 'He's a Shoshone Indian. He used to ride scout over at Fort Grant.'

'Where is he?'

'Drunk on his duff, last time I seen him,' the man answered. 'He claims to be a good tracker.'

'I thought it was against the law to sell whiskey to Indians?'

The man shrugged his shoulders. 'The Shoshone were always friendly to the white race, and he used to ride for General Crook. That kind of makes him one of the good guys.'

'You say this man was a scout for Crook?'

'Yep. Claims he was a head scout. He might be a help, once he's sober enough to see beyond the end of his nose.'

'I'll see about recruiting him in the morning.'

'Money talks,' the man replied. 'The guy spent every cent he had on whiskey tonight. If he can sit a horse tomorrow, I'm guessing he'll hire out to you.'

'What's your name, friend?'

'Rich Tyler,' he answered. 'I'm bartending at the Royal Flush casino. You need some help finding the Indian, give me a holler.'

'You know where he sleeps?'

Tyler laughed. 'Usually in the jail. He's only been around town for a few weeks, but he's learned there is always a free bed ready and waiting. With no sheriff, he has the place to himself.'

'Thanks for the information, Tyler.'

The mayor let out a long sigh. 'Hack was a long-time friend of mine. I'll go visit his wife and give her the bad news.'

'I'll put out a jar for donations at the casino,' Tyler offered. 'It's going to be tough on her, losing her man.'

Keene stood staring off into the night. Another man was dead. Worse than the attack, he'd actually assisted the killers in catching their victim this time. It was a great start for a special deputy marshal!

CHAPTER THREE

Rich Tyler met Keene at the jail the next morning. He showed him back into a cell, where there was a red-eyed, haggard-looking man, sitting on a bunk. He wore buckskin clothes, with a rawhide sash around his waist for a belt. A headband was around his forehead, with the rattles from a snake dangling at the back. His hair was cropped at the top of his shoulders, and he wore moccasins with deerskin leggings to his knees. His only weapon was a bone-handled knife.

'Razer,' Tyler spoke to him, 'this is Dorret Keene. He would like to hire you to scout for him.'

'I no longer chase Indians,' Razer muttered back. 'Let someone else hunt down the last of the free Indians.'

'We think these are white men, Razer. I'm sure you've heard of them,' Tyler explained. 'It's those Shadow Killers.'

The news caused the man to sit up straight. He put a gaze on Keene which was both alert and intense. It appeared to take some effort, but he stood up to face the two men. He was dark-skinned from the sun and had several different seasons of dust layered on his

40

skin. Obviously, a man who avoided contact with water, he was a head shorter than Keene, but he was stockily built. He appeared fit, with no evidence of extra meat on his bones.

'So you dare to seek out the evil spirits of the night, huh, Keene?'

'They killed a man last night. I intend to find out who they are and put an end to their vicious, murdering ways.'

Razer grinned. 'Maybe these Shadow Killers are Indian spirits, come back to cleanse the Territory of the white man.'

'The men I saw last night are flesh and blood, not spirits.'

'It could be dangerous, chasing after them – spirits or men.'

'Time's a-wasting, Razer,' Keene told him. 'The job pays two dollars a day. If you find me one of those raiders, I'll give you a bonus.'

'How much of a bonus?' Razer was all business.

'I'll donate a full quart of whiskey,' Tyler put in. 'It'd be worth that much to me.'

The scout stretched out his arms and emitted a prolonged yawn. Then he removed the headband and tucked it into his pocket. He retrieved a Navy Colt pistol and an old army hat from the foot of the bed. He placed the hat on his head and began to buckle on the gun.

'Let's get going, Keene,' he was practically impudent. 'But you need to get me a horse. I'm not going to walk.'

'You haven't got a horse of your own?'

Razer shrugged. 'I ran out of grub a few weeks

back. I ended up first selling the horse, then my saddle. I'm afoot and broke.'

Tyler laughed. 'Some scout you are. You ain't even got a horse.'

'Pick out one at the livery,' Keene told him. 'I'll pay the rental fee.'

Razer quickly exited the jail. It left Tyler alone with Keene. He used the opportunity to put a question or two to the bartender.

'Have you noticed anyone new arriving in town during the past week or so?'

The bartender shrugged. 'I've only been here a few months myself and landed a job at the casino. Have to ask someone else about strangers. I haven't learned all the regular faces yet.'

'You married?'

'I've been traveling too much to settle down, Keene. Maybe one day.'

'Me too.'

'You keep a sharp watch for those raiders. They are definitely a cold-blooded bunch.'

Keene said a farewell and hurried up to the stable. Mrs Shawn was already at the corral with Razer. A resourceful woman, she had to take over her husband's business as best she could. Evidence of her sorrow showed in the fact that her eyes were still red and puffy from crying.

'Mighty sorry about your husband, ma'am,' Keene told her gently.

She braved the words well. 'Our oldest son is able to take over most of the blacksmithing. We'll manage.'

'How much for the use of the horse?'

'We can settle when you return,' she said in a businesslike fashion. 'I figure you're good for the rental fee.'

He smiled at the elderly woman. Even with streaks of gray in her hair and age lines in her face, she was handsome. The inner strength was visible in her sober expression.

'Thank you, Mrs Shawn. We expect to be back in a day or two.'

'Catch them dirty sons!' she hissed through clenched teeth. 'Do whatever you have to, Mr Keene! But catch them!'

It was as close to an outburst of emotion as the woman had come. She regained her aplomb at once and walked back towards the stable gate. A pang of deep regret knotted up against Keene's heart. Why Hack Shawn? Why did the raiders brutally set fire to him? What kind of barbarous, utterly ruthless vermin was he up against?

Razer surveyed the ground and looked off into the hills. He gave a grunt of disgust and swung back up on to his horse. Keene rode up to him and awaited his report.

'These Shadow raiders leave prints like white men, but they are as smart as Indians. Their trail ends among the passing of a good many cattle along this range.'

Keene could see the brown dots of several head of cattle in the distance. They were in a small basin, with a natural pond from an underground spring. With all kinds of animals using the watering-hole, it would be next to impossible to follow anyone's trail.

'Any ideas?'

Razer shrugged his shoulders. 'I'm thinking this

job is only going to last one day. I can't follow the smell of individual horses.'

Keene looked closer at him. 'Speaking of smell, don't you ever get tired of having yourself around? I'd wager a bath would lighten your skin tone several shades. Make you a might easier on the nose too.'

Razer knitted his brow in thought. 'I had me a bath some months back.' He looked skyward, noting the scattered clouds. 'Might get me another one . . . if it comes on to rain.'

'What if we were to circle the basin?' Keene asked. 'Any chance you could pick up the trail of the two riders? I'm guessing they split up, after mixing their tracks with the herd of cattle. Any idea as to which direction they would go?'

Razer gave his head a negative shake. 'Take your pick, Keene. We're at the noose end of the rope here . . . it's a dead end.' He arched his back to relieve the stiffness and wiped his brow with the back of his hand. 'I don't know about you, but I could use a drink.'

'Is rot-gut whiskey all you think about?'

The man pondered a moment before answering. 'I sometimes think of fine horses or fair young maidens,' he said. 'I rode up on to five Arapaho women one time, when they were all sharing a bath in a secluded pool.' He grinned at the memory. 'Danged if I didn't fall in love with the whole, beautiful bunch.'

Keene grunted in disdain. 'You're a rotten example of a man, Razer, spying on women taking a bath.'

'Woman was made so man could enjoy her beauty, Keene.'

'They do have other worthwhile qualities, Razer.'

He grunted and got back to the original subject. 'What now?'

'Well, you didn't earn your beer today. I could have trailed those raiders this far on my own. I've seen every track and marking that you have.'

Razer bridled at his remark. 'You have not.'

'I sure did,' Keene replied sharply. 'I've seen everything you have.'

'No, you haven't!' Razer fired back testily.

'Oh yeah!' Keene retorted hotly. 'So, tell me, what have you seen with those keen, Indian peepers of yours that I've missed?'

'You're a hunter, not a tracker, Keene. You have eyes for only one direction. I'll bet you didn't even know we were being followed.' Razer curled his lips into a haughty sneer. 'Tell me you knew about the man back in trees!'

Keene was shocked down to his toes. He jerked around to look back the way they had come. The movement was what saved his life.

A bullet grazed his shirt-front and tore a path across the top of the pommel on the saddle! The distant boom of a big gun sounded as Keene rolled off the horse and landed in a crouched position. Jerking the reins, he yanked the animal around for cover.

A second slug kicked up dirt under his horse's belly. Keene saw the smoke of the gun-blast and heard the echo of the gun a second time. He fought for control of the frightened mount, then pulled his Henry rifle from the boot and jacked a bullet into the chamber. Aiming over the back of his horse, he sent several rounds into the trees in the direction of the ambusher.

The man beat a hasty retreat, unprepared to meet Keene on even terms. Through the scatter of brush and trees, Keene saw him gather up his horse and mount up. A moment later, he was lost beyond the ridge. Razer was still mounted, awaiting orders, by the time Keene managed to get back on to his own horse.

'Earn your keep, Razer,' he snarled. 'Follow that blasted bushwhacker!'

Razer was in motion at once, riding low over the saddle to make himself a hard target to hit. He rode directly for the last visible location of the ambusher. When he reached the spot where the rifleman had been, he slowed to read sign.

'Our shooter is not one of the Shadow raiders,' he said without the slightest doubt.

'What are you talking about?' Keene wanted to know. 'He saw us looking for tracks. You said the raiders had split up. It has to be one of them.'

But Razer continued to shake his head. 'No. This guy's horse has worn shoes, almost smooth from wear. Our killers from last night have horses with fresh iron.'

So who was it? Keene wondered.

Razer edged his horse up the trail, wary of a second ambush. The manner in which he remained draped over the front of the horse would have provided an extremely small target for a shooter, while it allowed him to scrutinize the ground for markings. Keene would have been stiff for a week to ride in such a position for five minutes. Razer remained that way for a full mile over rough and uneven terrain.

The rolling hills gave way to a mountainous

region, with deep gullies and steep ridges. The trees were a mix of piñon and spruce. There was creosote brush in the lower areas, with a tangle of scrub-oak lining the mouths of each ravine.

After winding through a brush-laden wash, Razer stopped at the base of a rocky escarpment and listened. Keene did likewise. A moment later, they were rewarded by the sound of shale rock being dislodged and rolling down the side of the precipice.

'There!' Razer whispered, pointing up the opposite bank.

Keene spotted the riderless horse. It was standing with the reins dangling to the ground. His prey was on foot.

'Let's get him!' he said, slipping off his horse.

'You hired me to track,' Razer said importantly. 'He's your problem now.'

'All right, blast your hide! You keep hold of the horses, while I go after him.'

Razer let him start off alone, but stopped him with a *p-s-s-t!* When Keene looked back at him, he grinned. 'If you don't come back, I'll take the horses as my pay.'

'Just don't leave until you're darn certain I'm dead, my unwashed pal, or I'll see you roasted over a low flame!'

Razer pointed to the upper end of the narrow gorge. 'He will be up among the rocks. He's using a big gun. Remember the sound.'

Keene didn't reply, carrying his own rifle at a ready position, moving quickly through the brush. Even as he worked along the wash, he thought about what

Razer had said. The gunshots had been deep and resounding. It had not been the explosion of a firearm like his Henry or a regular .44 rifle, but more the boom of a large caliber rifle. That meant the ambusher might have the advantage in range. He had to move in carefully. If the fellow opened up on him, he wanted to be close enough to return fire.

He took several steps, then paused to listen. He kept to the high brush and stealthily made his way toward the upper end of the deep wash. His heart was hammering, his palms moist, while his mouth was dry. He experienced a queasy roll in his gut, as he paused to catch his breath.

He tested the air for anything out of the ordinary, the smell of blood, body odor, the hint of tobacco. He didn't allow himself to stare at any single object in the distance, aware such a steady look would cause it to appear to move. He used his ears, while he kept his eyes moving, sweeping the terrain carefully. Every nerve was fully alert, each sense magnified to the highest degree of intensity. His finger slipped down to the trigger of its own volition. He could feel the man's presence. He was very close.

The body came hurtling through the air! Keene swung his rifle around, but he couldn't bring it to bear. . . .

The man's bulk struck him, knocking him over backwards. The two of them landed on the rocky hillside and slid downward in a snarl of arms and legs. When they hit bottom, his assailant was on top!

A knife arched though the air at Keene's head! He dodged to one side and the blade sank into the dirt next to his face. He locked his left hand on the man's wrist and the two of them rolled over. Keene recognized Zeke Hayden, as the hunter tried to drive the blade at him again. Only his quickness prevented Zeke from scoring a death strike. He twisted his body and managed to use his free hand to grip the man by the throat. Zeke didn't like that, thrashing about and kicking like a rope-entangled mule.

Keene shoved him away and jumped to his feet. They were poised against each other on the floor of the narrow canyon. Zeke flicked a glance around, as if he might try and make a break for his horse. Then he lunged at Keene again.

But this time, Keene was ready. He batted the knife out of the man's hand with a chopping blow to his wrist, then exploded a solid fist into Zeke's face. It knocked the hunter off balance. By the time he righted himself, Keene was fully on the attack. He pounded Zeke about the head with several punishing blows. A fist closed one of the hunter's eyes, another pulverized his lips to raw meat. When Keene delivered a right cross to Zeke's forehead, it knocked him off his feet.

Zeke rolled over twice and scrambled back up. As he came to his feet, he clawed for his handgun, jerking it from its holster!

Keene had started after him. He saw Zeke grab for his pistol and attempted to stop, while drawing his own gun at the same time. The result was his feet went right out from under him. He landed hard on his back pockets, just as he pulled the trigger on his Peacemaker. The gun bucked in his hand, a blast filled the air. . . .

Zeke had been ready to shoot, but he lost the pistol and threw his hands to his face. Then he pitched over on to his back, groaned once, and lay still.

Keene got up slowly, keeping a sharp eye on Zeke, but there was no further sign of life. When he checked the body, he discovered his bullet had hit the man at an upward angle between his nose and left eye. He'd died almost instantly.

Uttering a sigh of relief, he was also filled with a regret over having to kill the man, even if he was a bushwhacker. Another of Isaac's sons had been scoured from the scum of the earth. There could be little doubt the old man and his other son would be along one day soon.

Razer came on to the scene. He had picked up Zeke's horse and also been close enough to see the end of the fight. He approached with a half-baked grin on his face.

'You're a shrewd gunfighter, Keene.' He was chuckling. 'That's the first time I've ever seen a man use the strategy of falling on to his own backside in order to kill his opponent!'

'I got him didn't I?' Keene growled. 'It was a good shot.'

'You mean a *lucky* shot.'

'I'll take lucky, so long as I win the fight.'

'Well, you got him. I guess that's the main thing.'

'Yeah, and you were a big help. I don't know what I'd have done without you.'

'Hey! I followed your ambusher,' he argued. Then, pausing to take a closer look, 'and it's like I said – he ain't one of our Shadow spirits.'

'No. You were right about that much.'

'So, what's the story on this guy, Keene? Did you steal his money? his horse? his whiskey?'

'I took a woman away from him and his family. While I was at it, I happened to kill one of his brothers.'

'You killed a man over a woman?' Razer was incredulous.

'More or less.'

Razer sighed deeply. 'To kill for a horse – that I can understand. To kill for whiskey – I can also understand. But to kill for a woman? Why would you want the misery?'

Keene didn't bother telling him the girl was another man's woman. 'Help me load this character over his horse. We'll take him back to town.'

'We could bury him right here,' Razer suggested. 'I could take his horse.'

'I'm a deputy marshal, not a horse-thief.'

Razer laughed. 'From the way you handled him in the gunfight, you might do better to steal horses for a living.'

Keene moved over to Zeke's body. 'Lend a hand, funny man. We ought to make it back to town shortly after dark.'

'Yeah, OK, I only thought burying him here might save you from getting a reputation as a bad man with a gun.' Another of his grins. ' 'Course, that would be about right. You're pretty *bad* with your gun.'

'Speaking of *bad* – do all Shoshone make as many bad jokes as you?'

'You ought to be glad I even talk your language.'

'Yeah,' Keene replied with a grunt, 'that's a real bonus.'

*

Keene and Razer arrived back in town an hour after full dark. Keene grabbed himself a bite at a tavern and then headed for his room. Once stretched out on his bunk, he allowed his aching muscles to relax.

He'd killed a man, but was no closer to understanding the murders of the Shadow raiders. Their seemingly random killings made no sense. Every angle he worked up was a dead-end. The murdered men seemed to have very little in common.

Cowans had been sheriff, Billings was a banker, Jones was a farmer, Layton was a rancher and Shawn was a blacksmith. Three of them were original settlers of the valley, having come with the settlers from Ohio to start the little town. Their ages ran from young Billings at twenty-one to Joe Layton at fifty-two. In the war, Cowans and Jones had served with the Union forces. Layton and Shawn hadn't gone to war, and Billings was too young to fight. They were all upstanding citizens and had no feuds going with anyone.

'So what does that leave?' he asked aloud.

He considered the only possibilities. Three of the dead men had served on a jury several years back. However, young Billings was only in his teens at the time. Also, there was mention of a minute-man fighting force. They were the local citizens, organized to fight at a moment's notice, whenever there was Indian trouble. On record was a single skirmish with no loss of life. In that encounter, Shawn and Billings had not been present.

Keene gave up. Maybe he was trying too hard. He

would let the information filter about in his head and hope to see a glimmer of light. At this point in time, he didn't have a clue as to the who or why of the murders.

A knock came at the door. Keene sat up on the edge of the bed, pulled his Colt and asked: 'Who is it?'

'It's Tish Bonner, Mr Keene,' a female voice replied. 'Mr Tyler, the bartender, he sent to fetch you.'

Keene went over and opened the door. He still had the gun in his hand, but he didn't point it at the woman. When he caught sight of her, he recalled her at once.

'You're the lady who fainted the other night, the one with young Billings.'

She blushed shortly and ducked her head. 'I always had a bit of a weak stomach. When I realized who had been killed, I . . . well. . . .'

'No explanation needed.' He dismissed her reaction. 'What about Tyler?'

'I was walking past the casino, when he stopped me. He said I should come get you. We don't have a sheriff, you know.'

'What's the matter?'

'It's about that girl, the one who rode in with you?'

Keene practically sprang upon the woman, instantly concerned. 'What about her?'

She recoiled at his intense reaction, but held her ground. 'That dirty old man, Mr Clemons,' she said quickly, then ducked her head, as if embarrassed. 'He dressed her up in a bunch of petticoats and the like.' She squirmed uncomfortably. 'Now he's selling them.'

Keene paused to frown. 'He's doing what?'

'Selling the young lady's clothes,' Tish repeated, 'right off her back!'

Keene swore an oath and practically jumped into his boots. He strapped on his gun, shoved his hat into place and raced out of the room at a dead run. The young woman moved aside to keep from being trampled.

Keene dashed down the stairs and crossed the street. He recalled it was Saturday night, so the entire town was full of off-duty miners. They'd earned their three-dollars-a-day wages all week and were intent on having a good time. There was an acute shortage of women in this part of the country. Liquor and only a few females made for a good many fights. Keene hoped to avoid any trouble, but he left the thong off his gun, just in case.

Entering the saloon, he spied Clemons at once. The detestable skunk was on a platform, which was made up of three tables. Lyla was also standing before the crowd of men. Tears streamed down her face, as she clung modestly to a thin bodice and the last of a pile of petticoats. Even her shoes were gone.

'Let's hear it!' Clemons slurred the words, waving an empty bottle in the air. 'How much for the last petticoat?'

Before anyone could answer, Keene drew his Colt, paused a split second to aim, and fired. The bottle in the man's hand exploded and the ear-shattering boom silenced the entire gathering.

'Curse your rotten, stinking soul to hell, Cecil Clemons!' Keene snarled, shouldering through the crowd roughly. 'I ought to blow your head off!'

The man's face lost its color. He whirled about and tried to jump down from the table. He'd had too many drinks for that trick. He landed on his hands and knees. Before he could get away, Keene pounced on him.

'Wait!' Clemons cried, throwing his hands up to ward off any blow. 'Hold on, Keene!' He closed his eyes, expecting to be hit.

Keene waited, until Clemons opened his eyes. Then he nailed him flush in the nose with a solid punch! The man howled in pain and Keene took hold of his collar and turned for the door. Lyla was quickly down and grabbed her clothes into a bundle. As Keene dragged the blubbering man through the crowd, Lyla hurried after him.

The miners moved quietly to the side. The courtesy was due partly to Rich Tyler moving forward and holding a twin-barreled shotgun, ready for use. The excitement and thrill of the moment was lost. The men were more than willing to return to the gambling tables and drinking up their hard-earned wages. Keene didn't look like a fun man to tangle with, and Tyler held the shotgun as if he knew which end was dangerous.

When Keene reached the street he continued to drag Clemons to the nearest watering-trough. Hefting him up off of his knees, he shoved the drunk's head into the water! He held him and let him squirm under water for a long time. Finally, there was a rush of bubbles and he began to thrash about with both hands.

Keene jerked the man upward and watched him

gasp for breath. About the third breath, he shoved him under again. This time, he let him flounder for nearly a minute, before he yanked him out and threw him, face down, onto the ground. As the man drew in gulps of air, he bore into him with a murderous gaze.

'You listen to me, you sorry bag of guts!' Keene rasped, physically shaking from the desire to beat the man senseless. 'You're never going to come near Lyla again. Wife or no, I catch you within shouting distance and I'll rip your heart out by the roots and feed it to the first hungry dog I find! I mean what I say, Clemons! You don't have any claim on that girl – not any more.'

The man twisted and coughed from the water he'd swallowed. He turned his head and tried to rise upward. 'You can't do that, Keene! She's my wife! I traded for her!'

Keene put his foot on the back of the man's neck and stepped down, driving Cecil's face into the mud.

'Best clean out your ears, Clemons!' He hissed the words. 'The girl no longer belongs to you! I'm going to see to it she gets a divorce. Do you hear me?'

'C-can't do it . . .' he whimpered. 'She's mine! I paid for her.'

'You heed what I say, Clemons,' he warned him a last time. 'I'll get a judge to grant her a divorce . . . or I'll hang you from the nearest tree. Either way, you stay away from her!'

Leaving the man wallowing in the mud, he took Lyla by the arm and led her across the street toward the hotel.

'Why didn't you speak up for yourself?' He was a little too gruff. 'How did you end up on the table like that?'

Lyla was still sniffing back her fright and tears. 'I don't have any rights,' she sobbed. 'Besides, he said he would trade me to the Indians if I didn't do exactly what he told me to.'

'Cecil doesn't own you any more!' Keene snapped. 'I'll see to it!'

Lyla didn't speak again, as Keene led her back to the hotel. Tish Bonner was still waiting there, outwardly fearful over the excitement. To Keene's relief, she took hold of Lyla's arm.

'You poor dear,' she said gently. 'Let's get you upstairs in your room.'

Lyla had regained control of her emotions. She was still trembling from shame and fear, but did manage a glance at Keene. He read a mix of humiliation, gratitude and relief. He suppressed his rancor enough to force a consoling smile.

'Miss Bonner will see you get to bed all right, Lyla. I'll go back over and see you didn't leave anything behind.'

Lyla touched and held his hand in her own for a brief moment, then went along with Tish. He felt better, knowing another woman would be with her. Tish even looked about the same age as Lyla. That was bound to make her feel more comfortable than having a man fuss over her.

Keene returned to the casino a few minutes later. Tyler had put the tables back in place. They both took a quick look around, but it appeared as if Lyla had managed to grab up all of her clothing and accessories.

Tyler gave him a shrug. 'How about I buy you a drink?'

'Yeah,' Keene answered. 'A drink would probably be better for me than finding that miserable drunk and wringing his neck a second time.'

'The boys didn't know Cecil was being mean, Keene. She didn't object, so they figured it was all in fun.'

'Cecil threatened her, to make her go along.'

'The dirty old maggot. I should have sent for you right away.'

Keene swung a hard gaze over the miners. They were drinking and laughing, having earned some relief to their back-breaking work. He couldn't hold their actions against them. As Tyler pointed out, they didn't know that Lyla was up there against her will.

'I appreciate your help, Tyler. I don't know what I'd have done, if some of the miners had taken offense at my butting in.'

Tyler grinned, as he drew them each a beer. 'You'd have probably killed at least six of them right off. After you ran out of bullets, it would have been even money – you against the other fifty.'

Keene took a swallow and set down the glass. He narrowed his gaze at Tyler and asked: 'Do they have a judge in town?'

'Not since Judge Billings, Todd's dad, held the position. I never met him, he died a couple years back.'

Keene sighed. 'I aim to get the lady a divorce from Clemons.'

'Divorce is about as hard to come by as snake-lips, Keene.'

'I'm a deputy US marshal. I reckon I can get a judge to sign a decree or whatever.'

Tyler laughed. 'I'm for thinking you pretty much get whatever you want, Keene.'

'I told Clemons to stay away from her,' Keene told him, taking another sip of the beer.

'If you can't get one of them divorce papers, I'll hold the old skunk, while you put a noose around his neck. I'll even bring the rope.'

'I appreciate the support, Tyler.'

He shook his head back and forth. 'I can't imagine any pole-cat being so low that he would treat his wife with such disrespect. Does rot-gut whiskey cloud your mind to such an extent?'

'Only if you drink it.'

Tyler chuckled again. 'I'll remember that. From now on, I'll only drink if I'm alone . . . or with somebody.'

Keene took a last swallow of the beer, thanked Tyler for the drink a final time and left the saloon. He discovered the young woman, Tish, waiting at his door. She offered him a smile of greeting, but seemed uncomfortable. Perhaps she had some reservation about being face to face with a deputy marshal. Many people thought of such men as larger than life or little better than hired guns. He was unable to discern exactly what Tish thought about him.

The lady cocked her head toward Lyla's room. 'I wonder what your boss would say about you adopting that little orphan?'

'I didn't adopt her.'

'You'll excuse me for leaping to conclusions, but I distinctly heard you threaten Mr Clemons not to come near her again. That being the case, I assumed you were taking full custody of her.'

'I think she deserves more out of life than serving a man who bought her like a horse.'

Tish smiled again, as if she enjoyed teasing you him. 'Perhaps you would be wise to take the lady and leave Buckshot. Get away before the Shadow Killers think you are a threat to them. I'd hate to see a nice man like you get killed.'

'And what about the men the raiders keep murdering? Who's to stop them from killing more innocent people?'

A frown knitted her brow. 'You're only one man. You saw how they killed Hack Shawn. What if there are a dozen of them? What if they decide to stop you from snooping around? Where will that leave Lyla?'

'I was hired to do a job, ma'am. I'm not in the habit of starting something I don't finish.'

'What about Lyla?'

'I'm going to see about finding her a job tomorrow. It's my hope she can support herself and make a life of her own.'

Tish let out a sigh. 'Well, I put her to bed. She was pretty shaken by what happened.' Her gaze was suddenly intense. 'For what you are doing for her, I respect you, Mr Keene. I hope you don't get yourself killed.'

'Thank you, Miss Bonner.'

'If I can do anything else to help, I am staying with the Fettermans, out at their farm. I'm supposed to teach school this fall, if this raider business ever ends. With all the people scared to death, we haven't even begun work on the schoolhouse.'

'You make a mighty fine-looking schoolmarm,' Keene told her. 'Kind of makes me wish I was going to attend a few classes.'

The flattery produced a smile. 'The people of Buckshot are desperate. This would be my first year of teaching.'

'I wish you luck.'

'Don't wish me any of your luck, Mr Keene. I think you'll have need of it yourself. These Shadow Killers have proven how ruthless and dangerous they can be. I wouldn't want my name to be on their death list.'

Keene tipped his hat with his free hand, as the young lady wished him goodnight and left. His eyes followed after her, enticed by the subtle sway of her hips. Sweet, gentle personality, sandy blonde hair, deep-green eyes and a build like a sculpture's model. Young Billings would do himself proud to win the hand of Tish Bonner.

CHAPTER FOUR

Keene shaved and put on his relatively clean clothes. He sniffed at the stale air in his room and opened the window. He bundled up his dirty laundry and strapped on his gun. He paused to sniff the air again. This time, he didn't look at his own laundry. He knew he'd smelled that odor before. He yanked open the door to his room.

Razer fell right over. He'd been asleep! sitting on the floor and leaning against Keene's doorframe. The man's eyes popped open as his head bounced off the wooden floor.

'What are you doing here?' Keene wanted to know.

Razer rubbed the back of his head and sat up. 'Dang it all, Keene! why don't you knock before you open the door?'

'It's my door!' Keene snapped back at him. 'What are you doing stinking up the entire building?'

Razer paused from rubbing his head and put his nose in the air. 'I don't smell anything.'

'A skunk doesn't hide from its own scent,' Keene shot at him. 'But he doesn't have any friends either!'

Razer slowly got to his feet. His expression became indignant. 'I always figured a deputy marshal would have better manners, Keene. Especially with us being friends.'

'I don't recall saying we were friends,' Keene replied. 'If ever a man was looking for a fight, saying we were friends would be a sure-fire way to get one started.'

Razer chuckled. 'That's pretty good, Keene.'

Keene gave up trying to insult the man. It was impossible to find anything he could say which would offend the man's dignity. 'What do you want, Razer?'

'I'm as broke and hungry as a stray dog. I figured you would maybe hire me to go search the hills for those raiders. I'm the best tracker you'll find in these parts.'

'What happened to the five dollars I gave you yesterday?'

Razer shrugged. 'I bought some supper, a little something to drink, then I paid a couple bucks to buy a gal's petticoat.'

Keene glared at the smaller man. 'Don't tell me you were one of the lecherous perverts who were bidding on Lyla's clothes?'

Razer arched her eyebrows. 'Lyla? That her name?'

'Yes! and she was scared to death. What a miserable low-life lout! You actually bid on her clothing!'

Razer shrugged. 'I might be an Indian, Keene, but I like to look at a pretty girl, same as the next man.'

'I ought to serve your head up to Lyla on a platter!' Keene barked.

'I didn't see her putting up any protest!'

63

'Cecil forced her to go along with the auction. He threatened to trade her off to the Indians.'

'What makes you think the Indians would want her?' Razer replied. 'White women are nothing but trouble.'

'Now you're an expert on women?'

'I've never met one I would want to spend more than one night with.'

'But you enjoy looking at them undressed!'

'Well, yeah.' He showed a silly smirk. 'Most women are like a fancy present. They are the most fun and exciting when you get to unwrap them.'

Keene uttered a sigh of defeat. This was not a man with whom he cared to debate. They shared no common ground for rules.

Razer put his hands on his hips. 'What's the answer, Keene? You want to argue all day about ruffling a girl's dignity, or do we hunt down and capture those murdering raiders – the ones you were sent here to catch?'

Keene gave in. 'All right, you go hunt up those Shadow characters for me. When you find them, I'll make it worth your while.'

'What about a horse?'

'Take the one Zeke Hayden was riding.' Keene dug into his pocket and pulled out a couple dollars in change. 'Here's enough for breakfast and supplies for a day or two. Just don't go buying a bottle of booze with it.'

Razer's face lit up with a smile that projected an easy-come, easy-go attitude. His black eyes showed a kind of perverted, self-satisfied humor.

'You're not a bad sort, Keene. I'll be sorry to see the raiders kill you.'

'Thanks for the vote of confidence,' he said drily. 'Do you have any idea where to look for them?'

'Only the obvious place,' Razer replied smugly. 'The place where they are hiding.'

'And how will you know you've found the Shadow Killers?' Keene quizzed him again. 'They won't be wearing hoods or hanging a sign on their door announcing the fact.'

'Not to worry,' Razer said, pointing to his nose, 'I'll smell them out.' Then he left Keene's room and went down the hall.

Keene considered the wiseness of his decision, but mostly, he wondered if skunks could smell anything but themselves?

The door across the hall cracked open. He dismissed his malodorous pal from his mind, as he spied Lyla peeking out at him. It jarred him back to her situation and he moved over to stand in the hallway.

Lyla remained behind the partially open door, but there was a glowing warmth in her rich, chocolate eyes. Her coal-black hair hung loosely about her shoulders and, when he made eye contact, she exhibited a timid, but demure smile.

Keene put on his hat, trying to cover the feeling of weakness in his knees. Clemons's wife or not, he could not deny the urge to take the woman in his arms and hold her tight.

'I'd admire to take you out for some breakfast,' he said, fighting down the enamored impulse. 'Then, after I drop off my laundry, we'll take a turn around town and see if we can find a job for you.'

She pushed aside the door and stepped out into the hall, as sparkling fresh as a new spring morning. He offered his arm and, after the slightest hesitation, she took it. Keene felt his heart swell, being close to Lyla. He was growing very attached to this girl. Good or bad, right or wrong, he had to see she got a chance to start over, a chance to have a decent and full life.

Keene had no luck in finding employment for Lyla. The people were not outwardly rude to her, but each had an excuse for not needing any help. He put her to work on the information he'd gathered. She compiled several lengthy lists, using the history of each man, but it added nothing to his investigation. He was still missing the key, the one clue which would tie them all together. The only option was to add more information to their list. The dead men had to have something in common.

He first went to Mrs Shawn, but she could shed no light on her husband's murder. Next was a visit to young Billings, which also proved fruitless. His older brother had been the senior partner in the bank, but their father had left his holdings equally to the both of them. There had been no favoritism shown by the elder Billings upon his demise and the boys had always been close.

As for Sheriff Cowans, he had no family in Buckshot. He'd started out with the early settlers as a hired hand for Layton, then hauled freight for a living. He'd been sheriff for three years before he was killed.

Keene had drawn a total blank, when he rode out

to speak to the widow of Sam Jones. The farmer had left a wife and four kids behind. Fortunately, the children were all in their teens, so they were able to work the farm. The widow herself was as tough as the land and more hardy than the weeds which dared invade her private garden.

Mrs Jones was five-foot tall, with gray streaks throughout her light auburn hair. The eyes were unwavering and pale indigo in color. She wiped her hands on a worn apron and sent the kids out to the fields to work. It appeared that Keene's visit neither distressed or impressed her. He got the distinct feeling that here was a woman who had always taken whatever life threw at her and maintained her stride.

'I've got some fresh cider,' she offered, nodding toward a makeshift chair. 'You look a little dry from the ride out from town.'

'Thank you, ma'am,' Keene was cordial. 'I haven't had any cider in quite a spell.'

She poured each of them a generous portion and then sat down at the table opposite him. She took her time, taking a long drink and then shifting her weight to find a comfortable position on the wooden stool.

From the condition of the old shack and the tacky, crude furnishings, it was obvious the farm barely scratched out an existence.

'Figured you might show out here for a look,' she said, giving Keene a thoughtful once over. 'I heared there was a deputy marshal coming to Buckshot to solve the killings.'

'So far, I haven't been able to solve anything, Mrs Jones. If you don't mind, I have a few questions.'

'Speak your piece,' she offered. 'I want them murdering scum caught as bad as anyone in the valley.'

'Can you think of any possible motive someone might have for wanting Sam dead?'

Mrs Jones let out short sigh. 'You see what we got here, mostly dust and rocks. Can you see anything worth killing a body over?'

Keene rubbed his chin with the back of his hand. He figured this was another blank space in the information-gathering department. Every trail was a box canyon going nowhere.

'How about the past?' he asked. 'Was there anything Sam ever did that he regretted, any actions with the town people, any fighting or the like? Did he join in to run someone out of the country or possibly act as a member of a lynching party? Can you think of anything that happened which wasn't covered by the local newsletter?'

She again gave her head a negative shake. 'About the only thing my Sam done with the townsfolk was to sit on a jury. He was one of the men who sentenced a fellow to hang a few years back. That were the only time he ever sat on a jury.'

'I saw the coverage in the newsletter. It appeared most of the jury were original or long-time settlers of the valley.'

'Sam never talked about it much. He felt bad about sending a man to the gallows. Sam wasn't the kind of man to hurt no one.'

'Was there anything else, Mrs Jones? Did he ever ride with a posse or join in a fight or feud of some kind?'

'Like I says, Sam was a God-fearing man. He didn't

condone no violence. We left the people of Buckshot alone and they done the same to us.'

Keene thanked the woman for her time and the cider. Then he bid her good day and headed toward Layton range. He would check with Joe Layton's kids and see if any of them could shed more light on the puzzle.

That evening, Keene took Lyla to eat at the tavern. She was quiet during the meal and Keene didn't wish to force her into talking. However, he worried that she needed to open up and be more communicative. She had suffered through a nightmare existence, but it was time to heal and return to a life worth living. He decided to do a little coaxing, after they had finished.

'I'd like to visit with you for a few minutes,' he suggested, once they were back at the hotel.

She obediently followed him into his room. When he motioned for her to sit down on the bed, she did so without question. Keene took a seat next to her and studied her for a moment. She placed her hands in her lap and waited, head lowered enough to shield her eyes, opting not to meet his direct gaze.

'I sent off a wire to the US marshal today. I asked for him to look into getting you one of them divorce decrees. You are no longer the property of Cecil Clemons.'

'I-I've never known a divorced woman before. It isn't readily accepted.'

'Yeah,' he admitted, 'I know, but it's time you thought about making a life for yourself and becoming a part of society again.'

'I don't have any skills . . . except for cleaning or cooking.'

'God only gave each of us one life, Lyla. I reckon we all ought to make the most of it.'

She flicked a swift, inquisitorial glance at him. However, she lowered her gaze at once and wrung her hands together. Then, she took a deep breath and released it slowly, as if she had reached a decision.

'I-I don't know what to do.' Her voice was soft and childlike. 'I never let Cecil . . . I wouldn't let him touch me. He was often drunk and was older than my father. He made a few attempts to . . . consumate the marriage, but I fought him off. It often meant going hungry or sleeping on the ground, but I never gave in.'

Keene wondered why she would tell him such an intimate detail. He had not asked about her relationship with Cecil.

'You're a beautiful young woman,' he finally replied. 'You are sweet, gentle, kind . . . the type of girl most men would fight over.'

Her head lifted and a spark of fire entered her eyes. 'Until they learned I had been married to Cecil!' she said with some vehemence.

'And Clemons made you his personal slave.' It was a statement.

She answered with an up-down dip of her head.

Keene took hold of the girl's hand. 'I don't pretend to know the horrors you've been through, Lyla,' he told her in a kindly tone of voice. 'But I can think of nothing more tragic than for you to forfeit the remainder of your life. You are still a young woman. Most of your life is ahead of you.'

Lyla's lips were compressed, as if from her intense concentration. She wanted to believe what Keene was saying, but how did a person overcome such degradation and disgrace? How could she ever forget being married to Cecil?

Keene watched her, almost able to read her thoughts. He wasn't qualified to tell her how to forget the past. He didn't know the workings of a woman's mind or how she could ever cope with her memories. How did anyone convince another person of their own worth?

When she lowered her head, he knew his words had not been adequate. She would never really feel clean or unsullied. The humiliation was too great. Without actually realizing his own intentions, Keene put his hands to either side of the girl's face and lifted gently. He intended to look directly into her eyes, to show her he felt no reproach toward her for being a wife to a low-life slob like Cecil. However, she countered his action by closing her eyes. Whether shut to keep out his prying eyes or because she was brought to tears, he didn't know.

Whatever the case, Keene did not speak. Instead, he tilted his head to the side slightly, leaned forward and kissed her.

Lyla did not respond . . . nor did she pull away. Her lips remained tightly sealed, as if refusing his advance. Keene lingered a moment, feeling like an impetuous fool. If only he could. . . .

Then, like the slow warming of the morning sun, Lyla's lips parted ever so slightly and she returned a very delicate pressure of her own.

Keene hesitated with indecision. He would have enjoyed kissing her full and hard, to demonstrate his fondness for her. Yet, he feared that being overly aggressive would destroy her trust. While grappling with his own conscience, Lyla made the decision for them both. Her arms went around Keene's neck and she drew him close to her. The encounter was extraordinary, wonderful.

It seemed the room had been elevated to the heavens. Keene was overwhelmed by his own desires. He might have attempted to take the kiss further, but Lyla recovered her coolness. Her hands slipped down and she applied a light pressure to his chest.

Keene sobered at once and released her. The embrace was severed, the mood shattered by reality.

Lyla flicked a nervous glance at him, then hid her eyes beneath lowered lids. There was a crimson tint to her cheeks, but a softness in her voice.

'You are a very nice man, Mr Keene.'

He cleared his throat uncomfortably. 'I wasn't being nice just now. I shouldn't have been so forward, what with you being still married and all.'

'Yes . . . Dorret,' she murmured, 'I forgot my situation for a moment as well.'

'I hope you don't feel I was taking advantage of you,' he said. 'I wouldn't do that.'

Her head rotated from side to side. 'I think you were being very sweet. I-I almost felt like a lady again.' She laughed at her own statement. 'Well, maybe a slightly promiscuous lady.'

'I've never been accused of being much of a lady's man,' he said. 'In point of fact, I've never taken the time or expended the energy.' Then he gazed deeply into her resplendent eyes. 'Truthfully, I've never found a woman I wanted to impress or entice . . . until now.'

Lyla quickly shielded her eyes once more. 'I believe you,' she said, rising up from the bed, 'and I shall never forget this evening together.'

He watched her back away, moving toward the door. He knew better than to try and stop her, either with words or by physical actions. He had already gone way beyond what he had intended.

'Goodnight, Dorret,' she finished speaking, as she reached for the door.

'Yes, goodnight, Lyla.'

A second day of pounding leather, visiting friends and relatives of the Shadow victims, and Keene was no closer to discovering the motive behind the deadly attacks. The closest ties between the victims were two events which had taken place several years before. There was the skirmish with a band of renegade Apaches and the hanging of a man for murder. In either of the two instances, one or more of the victims was not involved.

Keene searched for any other aspects, too. Did someone gain a lot of wealth by any one person's death? Was the raiding a simple cover-up, a way of getting to any one or two men? It was mind-boggling, trying to piece together the single, complex puzzle, from all the sorted and wide variety of pieces.

Lyla worked tirelessly on the project. She included religion, politics, family origin and personal histories. Even with lengthy measures and comparisons, they discovered no concrete link between the murdered men.

Keene took her to supper that evening, feeling as if he had taken a road into a dead-end canyon. They were seated at a table, at the back of the hotel dining-room, when Razer came into sight. Lyla saw him first. She grabbed hold of Keene's wrist and pointed.

'Dorret!' she exclaimed. 'It's the Indian scout!'

Razer's clothes were covered with dried blood. He had rags tied about his wrists and there were several torn sections of his shirt and pants. He had one eye open only to a narrow slit, while the other was swollen completely shut. His face showed smears of blood and several dark bruises. Keene hurried over to him, before the man collapsed.

'Razer! What happened?' he asked, turning him around enough so he could inspect his injuries. 'It looks like you tried to get between two fighting grizzly bears.'

'You don't know half the tale,' Razer retorted. 'There were thirty of them, maybe more – men with clubs! They attacked me from ambush.' He held up his fists. 'I beat off the first fifteen or twenty of them, but then one of the coyotes hit me from behind. They dragged me over ten miles of rock, trampled me under their horses, then threw my broken body over a two-hundred-foot cliff.' He took a breath and continued: 'That wasn't so bad, but I landed in a lion's den. The old puma had two grown cubs and tried to serve me up for dinner. I had to kill them all with my bare hands!'

Keene uttered a grunt. 'You'll pardon me if I don't believe every detail of your story, Razer, but it's for certain you got a beating from some place. Let's get you over to the hotel and I'll round up the town doctor.'

'I don't want anything but sleep for about three days, Keene ... and maybe a bottle of snake poison for the pain. You don't have to make a big fuss over my nearly being killed ...' he uttered an exaggerated moan, 'although I was out there working for you.'

Keene took him to his own room and then sent for the doctor. The medico spent the better part of an hour with Razer. When he came out, he was shaking his head in disgust.

'Never seen so much dirt on one man in my life. I couldn't sort out where the skin ended and the weeks of built-up crud began.'

'How is he?'

The doctor grew serious. 'That beating would have killed a good many ordinary men. What happened to him?'

'You don't want to hear the story he fed me, Doc. I was hoping you could cast a little light on the subject.'

The man stuck out his hand. 'I don't believe we've met. I'm Rex Ragsdale. I own the tavern at the far end of town.'

'I've eaten there a time or two,' Keene replied. 'You're a doctor too?'

'I was a medic during the War between the States and was elected to be the town physician in Buckshot. My expertise doesn't go far beyond handing out a little pain-killer and binding a cut.'

'Dorret Keene,' he introduced himself to the doctor. 'I employed Razer to look for the hideout of those Shadow Killers. I'd say he stuck his face into a

75

hostile camp somewhere along the way.'

'Had marks of a dog bite on one arm and he had taken quite a beating.'

'Any permanent damage?'

'A couple cracked ribs, but nothing broken that either of us could tell. He did mention something about wanting you to get him a special kind of pain-killer.' Rex winked. 'I'll bet you know what he's talking about.'

'He sure earned his keep doing something,' Keene replied. 'I'll round him up a bottle after I get him some supper.'

'As you're the only lawman around, I guess you're safe enough making your own rules about serving hard liquor to Indians. I'll be seeing you.'

Keene handed him a couple of cartwheels as payment and then he returned to the dining-table. Lyla had waited patiently for him. She looked up expectantly for his report. He took a chair opposite her and told her what the doctor had said about Razer's condition.

'How did it happen?' Lyla asked.

'I don't know, Lyla. I guess you heard the cock-and-bull story he gave about his condition?' At her nod, he went on. 'The doctor said a dog had bitten him, and he'd certainly taken a beating. His wrists were raw from being tied with a rope. I'd guess he was likely caught snooping around a miners' camp and they worked him over.'

She stretched out her hand and placed it over his own. For some reason, it was the most calming action Keene had ever known. He smiled at the concern, which showed brightly in her face.

'I know,' he said softly. 'This Shadow business is getting risky as can be.'

CHAPTER FIVE

Razer was up and around the next day. Lyla had laundered his clothes until he was almost tolerable to be around. He griped about wearing clothes that smelled like a woman's soap, but they were all he owned.

Keene and Razer were returning from the livery when they were met by the mayor and Rich Tyler.

Fred Smith greeted them both with a wide smile. 'Like to speak to you, Keene.'

It didn't take much to savvy there was trouble in the man's friendly salutation.

'What's this about?' Keene asked, stopping to talk to the two men.

'I've a little proposition for you,' Smith spoke again. 'It concerns your lady-friend.'

'What kind of proposition?'

Smith looked at Tyler for help, but the bartender avoided his gaze. He was leaving the talking up to the mayor.

'Well, it seems that Bull McSwan is in town. He operates a mine some ten miles back into the hills. It ain't much, but he scratches out a little dust now and then.'

Keene narrowed his gaze. 'And?'

'Well, Bull is something of a troublemaker, Keene. Cowans used to lock him up nearly every time he came into Buckshot. He usually waited until Bull passed out from drinking too much. You see, Bull McSwan is a tough customer.'

'What's that got to do with me?'

Smith squirmed under Keene's hard stare. 'Well, it's like this, Keene. You're the only law in these here parts – until we find someone for the job of sheriff,' he added hurriedly. 'If you would handle Bull, it'd sure help us out.'

'I'm not looking to tangle with anyone with a nickname like Bull! What do you take me for, Mayor?'

'I thought we might arrange an exchange of courtesy.' At the skeptical lift of Keene's eyebrow, he continued rapidly: 'You've been trying to land your lady-friend a job, and we need a temporary town marshal.'

'It's only for a couple of weeks,' Tyler now joined in. 'We'll find someone for the job of sheriff pretty soon. And, in return, the young lady would have a permanent position working at the hotel.'

'That's right.' Smith hurried along with the offer. 'I'll give her room and board, plus two dollars a week to clean the rooms and do laundry. She'd be off every Sunday for church meetings and I'd only require her to work nine- or ten-hour days.'

'That's good pay for a woman,' Tyler put in enthusiastically.

'I can't be the town marshal – not for a few hours or even a couple of days. I've got another job to do here. How am I supposed to—'

'I'd be willing to help watch the jail for you,' Tyler spoke up eagerly. 'I don't know a whole lot about enforcing the law, but I told you before that I'm pretty good with a gun. You get any prisoners, I'll help tend to them on my off hours.'

'What do you say, Keene?' Smith pressed him. 'I'll raise the stakes and give your little lady-friend three dollars a week! With room and board, that's twice what she could make anyplace else.'

'It'd be a good job for her.' Tyler put in his two cents' worth. 'At least until she is divorced and a free woman.'

'Sounds pretty good to me, Keene.' Razer spoke through his swollen lips. 'You only have to be a lawman for a couple days and you get the girl a home and a job.'

'I don't need your advice, Razer. You can't even keep yourself out of trouble. I think you only want to see me mix it up with this Bull character so I'll end up as beat-up as you!'

Razer grinned. 'It'd be plenty fun to watch. Last time Bull came to town, I seen him break a hitching post with single punch. He's a tough *hombre* all right.'

'You think this is real funny, don't you?'

'I'd enjoy a good laugh, but my face hurts too much.'

'All right,' Keene agreed, 'but I've a few conditions about taking the job.' He turned to Smith. 'One condition is that you have an election or select a volunteer within two weeks to fill the position of sheriff.'

'Fine, fine,' Smith agreed at once.

'And second,' Keene went on, 'second, I'm holding you to the job for Lyla.' At Smith's eager nod, he allowed himself a wry grin. 'Lastly, I'll need a deputy to back me up. I want Razer sworn in to serve in that capacity.'

'No!' Razer cried. 'Hell, no!'

'An Indian?' Smith was also dumbfounded. 'You want an Indian for your deputy?'

'Yes,' Keene stuck to his proposition.

'That ought to cause a little stir.' Tyler laughed at the idea. 'Indians are real popular here in the south-west, what with a lot of Indian fighting still going on.'

'A Shoshone lawman?' Smith stated his concern about the idea again. 'I don't know if we can do that, Keene.'

'Those are my terms, Mayor. You can take them or leave me out of your plans. I'm not taking on the job of town marshal without back-up.'

'You really trust this man to back you up?' Tyler laughed at the notion. 'He's more likely to stand back with a bottle of red-eye and watch you get beaten like a dirty rug.'

Razer bobbed his head up and down. 'The bartender is telling it straight, Keene! You can't trust a red-hide Indian no more'n you can a cornered bobcat. I won't back you up. I won't!'

'You will, Razer,' Keene countered. 'It's the only way to see that Lyla gets a fair shake.'

The man's shoulders drooped and he hung his head. 'I swear, it's like I'm back in the army again. Everybody gives orders to the poor Indian!'

'All right, Keene,' Smith finally agreed. 'I accept your conditions. You're acting marshal and Razer is your deputy.' Then with a shake of his head. 'I hope you know what you're doing.'

The four of them walked over to the jail together. Smith had Razer and Keene raise their right hands and swore them in, with Tyler being a witness. Then the two new lawmen were left to discuss their duties.

Razer was first to speak. 'While I was recovering from my mishap, I looked over that pile of notes in your room. From what I could tell, you and your little female friend have covered every aspect of the Shadow Killers' victims.'

'And we've discovered nothing,' Keene admitted.

Razer rubbed his ribs tenderly, his face twisted in deep thought. When he spoke, it was as if he was thinking aloud. 'There *was* one new twist about the last killing. I think our raiders had to come into town for their victim.'

'What do you mean?'

'Take a look at the other murders,' Razer answered. 'All of the men resided out in the country. The killers always caught their victim alone and murdered him. Now they come riding right into town and kill their prey by dousing him with coal-oil and lighting him afire with a torch. They risk being shot or captured to get at Hack Shawn. A man has to wonder at the change in tactics.'

'Maybe Hack was the last man on their list. It could it be that the raiders have already left the country.'

'I don't think so,' Razer surmised. 'I think it's more likely that any of their remaining victims are here in town.'

'What if Hack wasn't their intended target?' Keene guessed. 'What if they picked him because he was alone at the time?'

'It could be. In fact, the raiders might be killing at random to keep us from knowing which men are scheduled for execution.'

'There's a cheery thought.'

Razer got back to their present situation. 'What do you intend to do about these new added duties? Mainly, what about Bull McSwan?'

'Maybe he won't cause any trouble this time, Razer. The man might only want a few drinks and do a little gambling at the faro tables.'

Razer tried to chuckle, then held a hand up to his swollen face. 'Ouch! Don't make me laugh, Keene. It's too blamed painful.'

'He's that predictable, huh?'

Razer nodded affirmatively. 'I was here the last time he showed up. From what I've heard about him, he always behaves the same way. He drinks for a time and gets good and mean. He'll either tear up the casino or start a fight. I heard about him once insulting a dance-hall gal. Two soldier-boys came forward to stand up for her. The gal ended up doused in a watering-trough and he chased the two blue-bellies around, driving them with a horse-whip!'

'And nothing was done about it?'

Razer shrugged indifferently. 'The soldiers outrun him, so he didn't hurt nothing but their pride. As for Bull, he passed out after about six laps around the casino. Then Cowans got the soldier-boys to help carry him over to the jail.'

'Sounds like Cowans let him run his course, rather

than try and prevent him from doing whatever he pleased.'

'You get a look at Bull and you'll understand Cowans's reasoning. The guy is twice the size of most men and has the temperament of a stepped-on badger.'

'I believe it's time for Bull McSwan to learn that laws were set down for all men to obey. You and I are going to teach him something about following the letter of the law and behaving himself in public places.'

Razer put a twisted, swollen grin on his mangled lips. 'Like to hear a dedicated lawman talk that way, Keene. I suppose you have an ace up your sleeve?'

'Yes, and it includes you.'

Razer glanced at the afternoon sun. 'We have several hours before Bull gets wound up. I'd say it will be a couple hours after dark, before he starts feeling his oats.'

'Let's see what we can accomplish in the meantime, Razer. No telling when those Shadow Killers will strike again. We need to formulate some kind of plan to catch them this time.'

'Good idea, Keene.' Razer tried to grin again. 'We solve this case and your only concern will be about that sweet little gal you took away from Clemons.'

It sounded good, but both of them knew they would have to have a change of luck. So far, they hadn't landed a chip on their side of the table. It was up to Lady Luck to smile on them – hopefully before another man fell victim to the Shadow Killers.

Keene watched the big man from the batwing doors.

No less than six-and-a-half-feet tall and weighing a solid 270 pounds, he would have made a fair-sized steer. The brute took a final swig from his bottle, stared at it for a long moment, then tossed it against the bar mirror. When the looking-glass shattered, Keene knew it was time to move in and confront him.

His logic was simple – a man only had to be half-prepared to engage in a battle of wits with a big drunken oaf like Bull. It was his size, not his brain, of which he would be wary. As he approached, the giant spun about, looking for a victim, someone to tear limb from limb. His eyes were red from drink, but his massive body was primed for combat.

Keene wasn't a small man, but he was dwarfed by Bull's massive frame. He stopped out of the man's reach and opened his coat to reveal the badge pinned to his vest. The action drew Bull's attention. In fact, the bruiser grinned, a wicked light dancing in his eyes. He had wanted a volunteer to chew up and eat for the evening dessert, and here was Keene, nice enough to sacrifice himself to appease his appetite.

'Before you do anything stupid, McSwan,' Keene warned him matter-of-factly, 'my deputy is standing behind you with a diamond-back rattlesnake.'

Bull froze, for Razer had silently slipped in behind him. He had the rattles from his headband between his thumb and first finger. As the room fell silent, Razer shook the rattles. It caused the blood to drain from Bull's face. He cocked his head slightly, enough to see Razer was at his back. He tried to pick him up in the reflection from the mirror – except he had just broken the glass into tiny pieces!

'You've been raising hell every time you come into town, McSwan,' Keene said tightly. 'The people hereabouts are getting real tired of your foolishness.'

Bull licked his lips and squared himself to Keene once more. Sweat trickled down his brow and he visibly swallowed before he could form any words. Snake or no, he wasn't the kind of man to back away from a fight.

'I don't scare, Mr Lawman. Bull McSwan ain't afraid of nothing!'

'Not even a diamond-back rattler?' Keene lifted his eyebrows in amazement. 'Not even a snake, whose bite will cause you to wither and die in unholy agony?'

Razer shook the rattles again, but Bull ignored him. He drew upon the reckless courage that comes in a bottle. His face was devoid of color, but he would not back down. He balled his big fists, raising them up into a fighting pose.

'Come on, lawman, give me your best shot – before I pound you into a lump of useless flesh. No one messes with Bull McSwan!'

Keene held his ground. But instead of accepting the challenge, he grinned. 'OK, big fella, but remember . . . you asked for this.'

Razer grabbed hold of the back of Bull's waistband and shoved something coiled and twisted down into his trousers!

Bull's eyes grew as wide as dinner-plates and he let out a bellow that would have done an enraged grizzly bear credit. He shouldered Keene aside and tore out of the casino on the dead run, knocking over chairs and a table *en route* to the street.

Keene and Razer followed after him, as did everyone in the casino. A number of people on the streets also gathered to see what was going on.

Bull darted about, like a man with hot coals in his drawers. As if that very thought occurred to him, he raced over to a watering-trough and sat down. He paid no attention to the laughter of his audience as he submerged his hindquarters deep into the water. He sat there, holding his breath, as if he was expecting to be struck by lightning. A full minute passed before he noticed the bemused look on Keene's face. Finally, he stood up and reached down deep into his soaked pants and felt around. What he came up with was a short piece of soft cotton rope. Realizing he had been made a fool of, his face darkened with a boiling fury. He threw down the rope, swore a bitter oath and glared at Keene.

'I'm gonna break you into small pieces, lawman!' He snarled the words. 'I'm gonna rip your arms from their sockets and then beat you with the bloody stumps.'

Keene tested the wind and reached into his vest pocket. He kept the evening breeze at his back, waiting for Bull to attack.

'You're through running roughshod over the people in Buckshot, McSwan,' he told the brute firmly. 'It's time you learned to behave like a gentleman.'

Bull threw the rope on to the ground at his feet and raised his beefy fists.

'You can stand and take it, or you can run!' he roared. 'Either way, I ain't going to leave enough of you for the ants or vultures to pick at.'

Keene was ready for the man's charge. When Bull started toward him, he tossed the handful of salt right into his face!

Bull gasped, as some of the granules of salt got into his eyes and burned wickedly. As the man blinked and backed up, Keene tossed the spice from his other pocket. Bull snorted and inhaled a dose of pepper. The seasoning assailed his nostrils and caused him to sneeze violently. He swung blindly at Keene, but he got only air.

Keene reached for more salt. When Bull's guard was down, he tossed it again into the man's eyes. The big man could only totter blindly about. Another dose of pepper and he was sneezing and gasping for air.

Keene grabbed hold of Bull and turned him around. The man swore vehemently and swung out wildly. His massive fist missed by a foot and Keene spun him around again. Each time he tried to rub his eyes or regain his wind, Keene was there to twist him about and toss more salt or pepper into his face.

Bull finally quit swinging and ducked his head, using both hands to try and rid the salt from his eyes. With the bully staggering and helpless, Keene pulled his skinning-knife. He stepped in behind the man and cut the suspenders which held up his pants. The trousers fell around Bull's ankles. Fortunately, for the ladies present, he was wearing his winter long johns. Everyone joined in to laugh and jeer at his predicament.

Bull grabbed up his pants, trying to keep them in place with one hand, while attempting to get the salt out of his eyes with the other. He was totally helpless against Keene's guiding hand – which landed him right back in the watering-trough!

With his knife still in his hand, Keene pinned Bull down in the trough. He placed the blade up under Bull's chin until the man ceased struggling.

'Are you a man of your word, Bull McSwan?' Keene demanded, jerking the man's head by his hair, shoving the blade hard against his neck.

'A-ain't no man ever dared call me a liar,' Bull managed to say.

'Then I want your word, here and now, in front of a hundred witnesses. I want your word that you'll never cause any more trouble in Buckshot!'

Bull was bobbing in the water, soaked from his waist down. With his eyes tightly closed against the sting of the salt, barely able to breathe without sneezing again, he was in no position to argue or balk.

Keene applied a bit more pressure to the knife, enough to draw a thin line of blood at his throat.

'Give me your word, Bull!' he commanded roughly. 'Give me your word or I'll cut through to your windpipe here and now!'

Bull had his teeth set. He didn't want to surrender. He wasn't a man who yielded to anyone. But then, he wasn't ready to die either. With all hope of resistance lost, he uttered a long sigh of defeat.

'All right, lawman,' he muttered, 'I give you my word.'

That brought a roar of approval from the crowd. Forgotten was the plight of the valley and the terror of the Shadow Killers. The only thing which mattered at the moment was that the large trouble-

89

maker, Bull McSwan, had given his word never to cause trouble in Buckshot again.

Keene withdrew his knife and dug out his handkerchief. He wet the cloth and helped Bull to wash the salt out his eyes. It took several minutes before Bull was able to stop the tears and see clearly. Then Keene gave him a hand out of the trough.

Bull stood with one hand holding on to his sagging, soggy trousers. He wasn't happy that he'd been bested without landing a punch. He looked down at Keene and anchored his jaw.

'I'd have whipped you in any kind of fair fight. You didn't give me no chance at all!'

'It's like you say, Bull, you'd have beaten me at any kind of fair fight. I didn't want a fight. I only want to avoid further trouble.'

'Rotten trick, sticking that piece of rope into my drawers,' Bull grunted. 'If it'd been a real snake and bitten me, ain't a man in the country who would have sucked out the poison.'

Keene laughed at the thought. 'The back of a man's lap is a tough place to treat for snakebite. I suspect it would have been difficult finding volunteers at that.'

Bull looked around and found Razer with his eyes. 'How'd you make that rattling sound, fella? I've heard a few diamond-backs make that very noise.'

Razer pointed to the rattles on the headband. 'The old boy didn't surrender these until I had taken care of the end with the fangs.'

'I owe you both a beating,' Bull grumbled. 'That was as dirty a trick as I ever heard of.'

'Time you were going home,' Keene told the big

man. 'There'll be no jail cell for you tonight.'

'Yeah, I'll go peacefully. You got my word. Bull McSwan ain't never gone back on his word – not my whole life.'

The crowd had dispersed back to their individual tastes. Only the three of them remained at the trough. Bull used a length of rope and made a belt for his pants. Then he left town without so much as another word.

'If only those Shadow boys could be handled as easily,' Keene sighed. 'I believe Bull will stay true to his word. I don't think he'll cause us any more trouble.'

'Got to hand it to you, Keene,' Razer allowed, attempting a crooked smile. 'That was a top-notch plan all the way.'

'Sticking that piece of rope into his pants is what made it all work. I guess he intended to drown the snake in the water.'

'What would you do, if you suddenly found yourself in the same position?' Razer asked. 'How *does* a man handle a rattlesnake in his drawers?'

Keene shrugged. 'I hope I never have to deal with that kind of decision.'

Razer attempted another of his pitiful grins. 'Me too, Keene. Me too.'

Lyla had waited up for Keene. He smiled at seeing her look of concern.

'You ought to get some sleep. You have to start work tomorrow – remember?'

Lyla remained in the hallway outside her door. She lowered her head, but didn't offer to go into her room. Keene could see something was troubling her. He tried to bring it out into the open.

'Is something the matter?'

She gave a negative shake of her head, but her ebony eyes flicked up at him with a trace of irritation. He could read most men at a glance, but never a woman. They didn't think in logic, but were driven by their emotions, their hearts. How was a man supposed to know how to comprehend what was in a woman's heart?

'What is it, Lyla?' He tried speaking softly, coaxing her with his voice. 'Is there something you want to ask or tell me?'

Lyla's head moved slowly from side to side, her long hair brushing over her shoulders from the gesture. Whatever was on her mind, it was not something she wanted to put into so many words.

Keene stepped closer to the girl and put his arms around her, pulling her gently to him. She came forward willingly, leaning against him and resting her head on his shoulder. They stood that way for a time. It was as if the girl needed a measure of reassurance or comfort. Keene didn't know exactly why or what for, but the holding her close seemed to be the right approach.

'You've had a tough go,' he murmured next to her delicate, cream-colored ear. 'I wish at times that I could read your mind. I would like to offer you comfort or understanding – whatever you need.'

Her arms encircled his waist and she pulled him more tightly against her. It occurred to Keene that she might have been concerned about his taking on Bull McSwan. Perhaps she was worried for him – not for herself. Maybe she needed. . . .

There suddenly came the sound of breaking glass. It was distant, as if at the other end of the hotel. A moment later, there came a muffled cry for help!

Keene pushed Lyla away. 'Get into your room and lock the door!'

She turned away to do as he directed, while Keene raced down the hall. He pulled his gun at the stairway, going down two steps at a time in a run. Jake was in the clerk's room, snoring blissfully. He hadn't heard a thing over the noise of his own slumber.

The ruckus emanated from the rear of the building. Keene hurried down the dark corridor toward Smith's apartment. He reached the door and could hear a scuffle from inside the mayor's room.

Putting his shoulder to the door, he crashed through and plunged into the dark interior. He vaguely made out two shadows – dragging a body in the direction of the window!

'Hold it!' he commanded, taking aim at the two figures.

But a third man slammed against him from the blind side. They went down together and rolled over. A fist struck him high on the forehead as he clubbed at the attacker with his pistol. His own aim caught the man low on the shoulder and caused him to jerk away.

The other two men dropped their load and made a hasty exit out the window. Even as they escaped, the third kicked Keene's arm, dislodging his gun. Keene rolled over to his hands and knees, searching for his Colt.

The choice to retrieve his gun was the wrong decision. The phantom only wanted to get away. By the time Keene located the pistol and turned after him, the man was diving out the window. Keene started to follow, but gunshots rang out and stopped him in his tracks. A dozen slugs hit the glass above the open window and tore through the opening into the room. Keene dropped for cover and had no chance to get off a shot of his own. When he heard shouts and the running of horses, he knew he had missed a chance to catch one of the intruders.

Keene put Smith on to his bunk and struck a match to his lamp. The old boy came around after a few seconds and gently rubbed a knot the size of a hen's egg on his skull. He groaned and sat up, about the same time as several of the townsmen arrived.

Keene explained what had happened. Doc Ragsdale moved over to the bed and began to examine the mayor.

'Easy, Fred,' he said, fingering the bump on his head. 'Sounds like you had a close call there. If Keene hadn't arrived in time to drive those men away, you might be dead now.'

Fred sought Keene with his gaze and located him standing over in one corner of the room. A look of utmost thankfulness flooded his aged face. 'Ragsdale is telling it straight. They had me,' he said hoarsely. 'Them raiders had come for my hide. One of them told me it was my time to die.'

'Did he say why?'

'No, only that I was going to die for my sins.'

'You probably will . . . but not tonight, Mayor,' Keene said. Then he let out a deep breath. 'I should have had one of them. I let him get out the window.'

'Well, you sure enough saved my life. I didn't figure to wake up again in this world.'

'Did you get a look at them?'

Smith gave a negative shake of his head. 'They had hoods over their faces and the room was dark. They were on me before I knew what was going on.'

'You were on their list, Mayor.' Keene stated the obvious. 'I want you to write your life history – right now, tonight!'

Smith sighed. 'I'll start right away. I don't know how it can possibly help, but I'll do it.'

'Got to be a reason, Fred,' the doctor said. 'If you're on the list, any of us might be next. We've got to learn why they want to kill so many people.'

'Every one of the victims has been an original settler in the valley or has lived here for a number of years.' The doctor thought out loud. 'You don't suppose we built the town over a sacred burial ground or something?'

'I know one thing,' Keene replied to his suggestion. 'The man I hit was no spirit or phantom. He was flesh and blood. Another thing, he didn't want to stick around and fight me on a one-on-one basis. These characters are human, but they don't like even odds.'

'But why me?' Smith spoke absently. 'Why should they want to kill me?'

'We could put forth the same question concerning all of the victims up to this point. Why have any of them been killed and how do they tie in together?'

The doctor paused to look into Fred Smith's eyes and grunted. 'You might have a concussion. If you feel dizzy or weak by morning, better remain in bed for a couple days. If you feel all right, you can get back to rolling drunks in the alley and robbing your customers blind.' He grinned, trying to lighten Smith's mood. 'Instead of asking who would want to kill you, we ought to be narrowing down the field of those who wouldn't. Be a lot less to count that way.'

'You're a big help, Ragsdale,' Smith grumbled. 'I'm about get killed and you use your cheap bedside humor on me!'

'If you think it's cheap, wait until you see my bill.'

Keene left the two of them bantering back and forth, like two dogs bragging about who could bark the loudest. The medicine Doc Ragsdale provided was the best kind he could have prescribed. His repartee with Smith would help calm the mayor's nerves and take his mind off of his near abduction and inevitable gruesome murder.

Keene returned to his own room, stopping first to tell Lyla that everything was all right. Razer arrived, as Lyla was closing her door.

'What's been going on?' he asked.

'Where have you been?'

Razer yawned. 'I was asleep in the jail. Next thing, I hear some shooting out in the back of the hotel.'

'You didn't get a look at them?'

'At them who?'

'Some scout you are,' Keene griped. 'Those Shadow Killers could have burned the town to the ground and you wouldn't have been rousted from your sleep.'

'Been around civilized people too long.' Razer

96

excused his lack of vigilance. 'I'm starting to pick up their bad habits.'

'We've got a new set of tracks to follow tomorrow.'

'Right into a herd of Layton cattle,' Razer replied. 'There'll be no trail after that.'

'I'm getting real tired of those killers making fools out of us.'

'Their hideout is probably a deserted shack or one of the mines, but which one and where?' Razer pointed at his discolored eye. 'Last time I went looking, I got myself strung up like a side of beef.'

'What happened to the thirty men with clubs.'

'Yeah, well that came later.'

'Sounds like another point against you, Razer,' Keene teased. 'You're supposed to be a master in the art of stealth, yet you admit to getting caught while snooping.'

'Where did you get all of your information, Keene? Since when did a city boy from back East become an expert about Indian scouts?'

Keene grinned. 'Silly me. I listened to the stories about you. I was told you were the best scout around.'

'They maybe should have told you I was the *only* scout around!'

'They missed tonight.' Keene grew serious. 'That's a first for them.'

'At least we know they're still around.'

'And they came into town for Smith. Your guess about them running out of victims in the outlying areas is beginning to hold water. The question is, how many more are on their list?'

'Smith could be the last one,' Razer suggested.

'Being one of the more prominent citizens, maybe they wanted to save him for the final victim.'

Keene racked his brain. 'But why Smith? Why any of them?'

'Smart lawman would have captured one of those men and we would have made him talk. Letting them get away was real careless.'

'Thanks,' Keene said drily. 'It did occur to me to stop one of them, even if I had to kill him, but I didn't get the chance.'

Razer grinned broadly, the shoe being on Keene's foot now that he'd turned the blunders toward him. 'I guess you couldn't find a place where you could fall on your rump, while you were shooting. I've seen the way you win a gunfight – remember?'

'You're a real funny man, Razer. Why don't you go look up those fellows who about beat you to death? Maybe they could get the job done right this time.'

Razer gave an indignant grunt. 'I'll see you in the morning. I'm going back to bed.'

Keene did the same thing. He went into his room and tried to go to sleep. However, his mind wouldn't allow him to relax. He kept going over each victim in his mind again and again, trying to link them together. The more he thought about it, the more he believed these murders had to be revenge-motivated. It was the only answer to make sense.

What's the common denominator? he wondered. What secret did the victims share? And how did Smith fit into the puzzle? There had to be answers, and he needed to find them, before the raiders killed again!

CHAPTER SIX

Todd Billings was visiting with Smith when Keene arrived to pick up his notes. The young banker's face showed a deep concern.

'Talk about a close call, Keene,' he said, tipping his head in the direction of the boarded-over window. 'When those raiders come right into a man's house after him, the time has come for action!'

'I'm game to do just that, Billings, but how do you suggest we go about it? We've still no clue as to who we're after or why they are killing people.'

'Just what are you doing?' Billings wanted to know. 'The Shadow killers murdered my brother out at our little ranch, so it's a certainty I'm also on their death list. The whole town is in an uproar. No one feels safe any more.'

'Razer is out looking for sign, but the raiders always make for Layton's range. We've had no luck following their tracks, after they mix in with a hundred head of cattle.'

Billings rubbed his hands together nervously. Smith was sitting up in bed. He looked well enough to be up and around, but bed probably seemed a safer bet.

'Have you got any clues at all?' the mayor asked carefully.

'There is no pattern to follow, Mayor. Their early victims were all men who lived out in the country, but they came into town after you. That might mean the remaining people on their list live in Buckshot. You'll recall Hack was out on the main street.'

Smith thought about that. 'And all of the men killed were long-time settlers here.'

'Yes, which indicates this could be a vendetta from something which happened a long time ago.'

Smith frowned. 'I suppose you could be right, but there are at least six or eight more of the settlement's original colonists still living outside town. Why not them?'

'Precisely why we're getting nowhere with the investigation. There has to be a common bond which ties the list of victims together.'

'I don't know about anyone else,' Billings declared, 'but I think the time has come for us to defend ourselves! I've hired myself a guard. All of the attacks have taken place at nights, so I'm putting a man with a gun right outside my house.'

'Who'd you hire, Todd?' Smith asked.

'J.T. Reynolds. He's been working at the Little Star mine for wages. I don't pay as well, but he doesn't have to work underground either. With him outside and me with a gun at hand, those Shadow Killers had better think twice about trying to take me out.'

'We can't all hire men to guard us at nights,' Smith

said. 'Next thing you know, our guards would be shooting at one another. If some kid were to light a firecracker there would be guns popping off all over town.'

'You do what you want, Mayor. I'm not going to end up being dragged out of my bedroom window.'

Keene stood in silence and watched the young man leave. Once his steps had faded down the hall, he removed his hat and scratched his head. 'Reynolds.' He repeated the name of the guard Billings had hired. 'Why does that name ring a bell?'

'You grabbed his horse the night Hack was killed,' Smith reminded him.

'Yes, but there's something else,' Keene replied. 'What do you know about him?'

'No more than I do about most of the miners. He comes into town once in a while and spends a little money at one of the casinos. He's never caused anyone trouble and seems a nice enough sort.'

'I think I might have seen the name in my notes.'

'Nothing too uncommon about his name. How many Smiths have you come across?'

'Yeah, you're right on that point.'

'Besides, what man would come here to kill a bunch of us and use his real name – especially if the name linked him to the murders?'

'I guess I'm grasping at anything that floats, Mayor. A man does that when he's drowning in a sea of murder and mystery.'

'I'm confident you will solve this case pretty soon, Keene. I know you've got the brains for the job. All you need is a break.'

Keene sighed. 'I'll get them all right, Mayor. But I'd like to do it before they kill again.'

'I'll second that motion . . . particularly when I've been nominated to be their next victim!'

Keene left the hotel and was about to cross the street toward the jail. He wanted to look for the name of Reynolds, and he had moved a good portion of his paperwork to the office. His room at the hotel was too confined and had only a single window. From the jail he could sort through the papers and study them during the day, while still being able to keep an eye on the rest of town.

Even as he reached the porch, he paused to automatically undo the thong on his gun. The hair seemed suddenly to become erect along the back of his neck. He was not wearing a jacket, only his vest and long-sleeved shirt. However, it wasn't the crispness of the morning air which caused the prickle along his spine.

'They say some men have a sixth sense.' A cool voice spoke from the alleyway between the hotel and the next building.

Keene swiveled around to see a stranger move out into the open. His blood jelled in his veins, just from looking into the man's eyes. They were dark and somber, like those of a snake, yet alert and penetrating.

'I'm Link Casto, Marshal,' the gunman said easily, spreading his feet to a comfortable stance. His hand was poised over his gun, deadly, menacing.

Keene moved ever so slowly, continuing around to face him squarely. His heart stopped, his stomach rolled over and his breath was suddenly short and rapid. His knees felt as weak as warm butter, while his hand automatically lowered above the butt handle of his own gun.

'What can I do for you, Casto?' His voice sounded much stronger than he felt.

'I'm one of the Shadow Killers, Keene.' The words were uttered softly, barely reaching Keene's ears. 'I wanted you to know that before I kill you.'

It was a moment which stopped time itself. All sounds, all sights, all sensations were lost. Keene knew only one certainty – he had to kill Link Casto or be killed himself. To let the man draw first would assure his own death. His only edge would be to make the first move for his own gun.

'You're a Shadow Killer?'

The lines in the man's face grew contorted with a hideous sneer. Bloodlust was naked in his expression. Here was a man primed to kill. 'Time to die, Mr Lawman,' he rasped. 'You aren't going to interfere again.'

'Why are you murdering the people of Buckshot?' Keene asked, trying to break the man's concentration. 'What possible motive is there behind these attacks?'

'No need to tell a dead man,' Link replied confidently. 'I don't think—'

Keene didn't wait for him to finish, desperately grabbing for his gun. He jerked the Peacemaker free from the holster as Link cleared leather with his own gun. The man's movement was a blur. He was much faster than Keene. They would both die!

The buck of the Peacemaker in Keene's hand was simultaneous with the blast from Casto's pistol. It seemed the raider's gun exploded in Keene's face.

There was a tremendous shock, as a white-hot object passed right through Keene's body. It knocked him back a full step. But instead of going down, he called upon his instincts to pull the trigger a second and third time. . . .

The sound of gunfire detonated within Keene's head. His sight was lost to an ocean of black. The waves swept over and engulfed his senses. He was dragged down into the dark, murky depths of a cold, ink-black sea.

From somewhere, there came a distant shout, but Keene couldn't hear the words. He felt the porch under him, as his head bounced off the wooden planks. Then his consciousness was overwhelmed by frothing, black whirlpools, which sucked him deep into opaque waters that blocked all light and sensations.

So this is death? was Keene's final impression. Then he was lost to the infinite void, free of worry or pain.

Keene's eyes were locked tightly closed. It was as if rust had corroded the lids until they were warped and jammed shut. He was in a world of eternal blackness, lost in an insensate limbo. Assorted dreams and weird images passed in front of his mind's eye, but he could not rouse himself to awareness.

There was an odd sense of presence, the pressure of a moist hand or cooling dampness against his brow. Then the momentary impression was lost to the oblivion of the black void once more. He bobbed helplessly in the dark ocean, comatose, swallowing gallons of tasteless waste, flailing with paralyzed arms within the torpid waters. His world was not real, yet it was still part of reality. Keene's fogged brain sparked enough to form broken thoughts: *If this is death, am I in heaven or hell? Are there any fish in these waters? Why do I feel pain? Is there a rotten smell to to the sea, or is Razer close by?*

A gentle hand caressed his cheek and a cool moistness was again on his forehead. He renewed his struggle to find a path out of the murky, lethargic waters, and was finally rewarded by being washed ashore. He was back with the living, breathing and aware of the world around him once more.

His eyes pried the corrosive doors open to tiny slits. His brain screamed from the shock of the piercing, knifelike rays of light! As he began to focus, he discovered a small, oval face above him. Concern and worry showed brightly in Lyla's face.

'H-hello, my taciturn beauty.' A hoarse whisper reached his ears. It was something of a shock to realize it was his own voice.

Lyla quickly produced a glass of water and put it up to his mouth. Keene managed a few sips and felt the dryness of his throat dissipate. He ran his tongue along his lips and found them chapped and dry. It came as no surprise that he didn't have the strength to raise or move his head.

'Have I been out long?' he asked.

Lyla laid a hand alongside his cheek and stroked it gently. 'Three days,' she answered.

'Three days!' he declared. 'That's why I feel as weak as a newborn kitten. What about the other man – Link something, he called himself.'

Lyla gave a shake of her head. 'He was buried yesterday,' she informed him. Then she began to mop Keene's forehead with a damp cloth.

'I suspect I've been something of a burden, haven't I?'

She offered him a slight smile, curling her sinuous lips at the corners. However, she gave her head a negative shake.

'And you've probably been looking over me night and day, haven't you?'

'I've spent a little time with you.'

'You can get some rest.' He grew serious. 'I'm going to be fine.'

That brought another negative shake of her head. Her eyes were red from lack of sleep, there were lines in her face from worry, and she moved stiffly, as if she'd been sitting at his bedside for hours on end. Still, she wasn't going to be ordered away from her nursing station.

'Really, Lyla. I feel pretty good. Why don't you take a little time for yourself and relax. Get some sleep.'

'I'll be right back,' she told him, ignoring his suggestion. She left the room, but it was only to return a few minutes later, with a bowl of hot broth and a cup of coffee. As he was too weak to resist her efforts, he had to let her feed him like a baby.

About the time he finished the hearty meal, the mayor arrived. He waited until Lyla left with the dishes. Then he peeked out from behind the curtain, looking out the window. After a moment, he turned back to Keene.

'Thought we might lose you for a spell, Keene,' he said. 'Old Ragsdale was sure glad to see the bullet had gone clear through you. He said you'd have died otherwise. I don't think he has much confidence about cutting into a man to dig out a slug.'

'What did you find out about the other man? He was one of the Shadow Killers.'

Smith raised his eyebrows in surprise. 'He admitted it?'

'Right before we shot it out. He told me his name was Link . . . Link Casto.' Keene recalled the name, thinking back to the deadly, cold-eyed, steel jawed man. 'He said he didn't want me interfering in their plans again.'

'He undoubtedly knew you were a lawman.'

'Enough so he called me by the title.'

Smith removed his derby and scratched what little hair he had right on top of his head. Then he turned the hat in his hands, working his brain.

'They must have someone in town aiding them. They knew when to hit Hack, they knew where to find me, and they know you are a deputy US marshal. They have eyes and ears right here in town.'

'So it would seem.'

'But who? Who could it be?'

'More than that, Mayor, we still don't know why. Are you sure you're not all hiding some deep dark secret from me about the town?'

'If there is a secret, it's one I don't know about, Keene. Everything any of us can remember happening is in the notes we've given you. I'm as much in the dark about the attacks as you, and I'm the one who needs to worry! Knowing I'm on the killer's list, I'm even more anxious than you to discover what's behind all of this.'

'Anyone in town admit to knowing or ever seeing that Link character?'

'Nary a soul. He had a horse with a Colorado brand on its hip, but it isn't from any ranch I recognize. I sent off a wire to Denver, to see if the brand is registered, but it'll take some time to get an answer.'

Keene took a deep breath and felt a sharp stab of pain near his upper chest. It spread outward to below his left shoulder. He felt stronger already, but it would take time to heal.

'Where did I get hit?'

'Above the heart and slightly to the left. The exit was under your shoulder blade. You were real lucky that it missed your lung.'

'Have you seen Razer?'

'He just arrived back in town this morning. I imagine he'll be around to see you. I don't think he's found anything yet, but he didn't get beaten half to death on this trip.'

'Man isn't doing his job if he isn't covered in blood.'

Smith chuckled. 'If I see him, I'll mention his lack of devotion to the job.'

Lyla returned to the room. She had a fresh pitcher of water and a towel. She gave Smith a warning frown.

'I'd say my time is up,' the mayor deduced from

the sharp look. 'The little worry-wart here has been at your side every minute. It's a wonder she even let Ragsdale tend to your wounds.'

Lyla stuck out her arm and pointed a finger at the door. The stern look on her face caused Smith to head that direction.

'I'll see you tomorrow, Keene.' Then with a frown at Lyla. 'You might ask your nurse if I can stay a bit longer!'

'Out!' Lyla spoke the word forcefully.

'Yes, yes, I'm going!'

Keene would have laughed, but he knew it would have been much too painful. He decided the best course of action was to lie back and enjoy being pampered. The case at hand would have to wait . . . at least, until he had recovered enough to get out of bed.

CHAPTER SEVEN

The next day, Keene was able to sit up with the help of a couple fluffy pillows. He could see out his solitary window, but there wasn't much to look at. He wished he had been put up over at the jail. At least the office there had a full view of the main street.

Lyla had stacked the piles of notes next to the bed on his right side. He suffered a little discomfort each time he used his right hand to stretch or reach, but he was able to feed himself and do a little work. He was forced to keep his left arm pinned to his side to relax the ache in his chest. Any movement with that arm sent streaks of pain shooting through his entire body.

Keene used the resting period to think, to try and figure the reason why the Shadow Killers were attacking and murdering only certain victims. There was a common denominator, there had to be.

His thoughts returned to Link Casto. The memory of facing off against the man filled his very being with renewed dread. He relived the split second again in his mind. He could see the muzzle of the man's gun, feel the hot piece of lead as it pierced through his body. There was smoke, fire, and the incredible shock of being hit. The aftermath of the dreaded vision was a world of darkness and lying near death's door.

To get his mind off the event, he reached out and sorted through the papers. He'd gone over and over the facts, the stories, the histories. He was missing something. The clues were right here. All he had to do was uncover a few meaningful facts.

His eyes rested on the account of the skirmish with the Indians. The battle had been between a dozen renegade Indians and the minute-men militia from Buckshot. It didn't seem to warrant any concern, let alone a likely foundation for a string of murders. After all, no one was even killed in that short encounter. True, most of the victims had been in on the battle, but these Shadow Killers didn't behave like Indians, and Link Casto didn't look to have Indian blood. No, he could see nothing to implicate any renegade Indians.

On the next page was the closest thing he had to a tie-in with all of the victims. It was an editorial covering a trial that had taken place in Buckshot some five years earlier. He paused to give it some hard consideration.

Cowans hadn't been sheriff then, but he had sat on the jury. Joe Layton and the farmer, Jones, had also been among the jurors. But what about Hack and Billings? He continued to read and look it over again. Then he paused to look at the summary of the testimony given. The name Hack Shawn appeared! He had been called to testify as a witness!

Keene's heart began to pound. The trial involved four of the five men! Smith was number six, and he had also been a member of the jury. That left only young Billings as not being a part of the trial. Could it be that Todd's brother was killed by mistake, or perhaps to throw people off the scent?

The man on trial had been hanged for murder. His name was Vin Hollis. He'd killed a local man in a card game. The newsletter didn't supply much actual information about the trial, but Smith had been a juror. He might shed a little light on the matter.

Keene shut his eyes, trying to put together a formula that made sense. If he took Billings out of the equation, the murders were definitely related to the hanging of Vin Hollis. His first chore would be to send off some wires and do some checking on the man's background. It might be that. . . .

His eyes popped open at once. He heard a man curse in the hallway. There came more noise, like a scuffle of some kind, then the sound of a glass or jar hitting the floor.

Lyla suddenly appeared in the doorway, but a hand shot out and grabbed her from behind. She uttered a gasp for help, but was dragged away. Keene rose up stiffly in bed, as he caught a glimpse of old man Clemons. He had come for Lyla!

Keene swung his feet over the edge of the bed and grabbed his trousers. Using his good right arm, he jerked the pants on, then staggered for the door. Waves of pain scorched through his chest and left side. He set his teeth against the burning fire and forced his feet to take him out into the hall. He came upon Lyla, struggling against the much bigger, dirty and unshaven man.

Cecil had a hold of her hair and also had one of her arms twisted up around behind her back. Lyla was not much for size, but she was putting up a good fight.

'Damn your hide, gal!' Cecil cried, wrenching her arm until she sucked in her breath and grimaced in pain. 'Quit your fighting me!'

'Turn her loose!' Keene snarled, moving unsteadily toward the two of them. 'So help me, Clemons, I'll break your filthy neck!'

Cecil glowered at Keene with hot, smoldering eyes. He surmised how weak and feeble Keene was from his injury. It gave him a sadistic confidence. With a violent toss, he threw Lyla down on to the floor. Then he came at Keene with his fists poised for a fight.

'All right, you meddling tinhorn!' he bellowed. 'Try to steal my wife away from me, will you? I'll teach you a lesson you won't soon forget!'

Keene was stiff and slow, but still ducked the man's first, wild, roundhouse punch. He countered at once, lashing out with his right hand. His knuckles rapped Cecil right in the mouth, crushing his lips against his teeth. However, the punch cost him dearly, as pain exploded within Keene's chest from the jarring contact. He groaned and doubled over from the shock waves which ignited to rip his body in two.

Cecil spat a mouthful of blood and started swinging. When he made impact with Keene's chest it drove him backward into the wall. He was consumed by a raging fire that burned throughout his entire body. He covered up, protecting the injury, but unable to defend himself.

Lyla didn't sit passively by and watch him take a

beating. She flung herself on to Cecil's back and grabbed on to him with both hands. He had to throw her off bodily. Then he slapped her hard enough to knock her down.

Keene couldn't find the strength to tackle Cecil with his fists. He turned for his room, filled with a bitter rage. If he could reach his gun, he'd kill the dirty, vile animal.

But Cecil wasn't fool enough to forget about Keene. He caught him from behind and tackled him. The jolt from the punishing contact took Keene's breath away. He doubled up in agony.

Cecil began to slug and pound away at him. Keene went down, desperately trying to keep his arms in front of the wounded left side of his chest. Keene could not withstand Cecil's assault. The darkness loomed within his mind, blocking out his reasoning. He let go of consciousness, fearful that death was waiting in the blackness.

Lyla almost ran right over Razer. She had been racing out of the hotel at full tilt and met him at the door. Before he could ask what was the matter, she grabbed him by the arm.

'Come on!' she ordered, dragging him back into the hotel with her. 'Hurry!'

Razer followed quickly, afraid Keene had suffered some kind of lapse, that he might be unconscious and dying. Then he saw Cecil, just as the man kicked at the inert body at his feet.

Razer broke loose from Lyla's hold and charged into Clemons like a bull. His head butted into the man, knocking him staggering down the hall. Before he could recover to figure out what was happening, Razer slashed out with a wicked right hand and squashed the man's nose.

Clemons howled in pain, but his cry was cut short by a second blow to the face. He backed away, futilely trying to defend himself. He had no chance against Razer. He was rocked by the vicious attack, pummeled by an endless number of solid blows to the face and body.

Razer mangled the man's lips with a solid left, then stunned him to his toes with a right to the jaw. Cecil flung up his hands, to cover his face, desperate to escape the deadly assault. He retreated until he reached a window at the far end of the hall. He would have stopped there to take a beating, but Razer hit him so hard, he was knocked backwards into and right through the window!

The pane shattered and Clemons fell from the second story. He landed on a pile of garbage, which had been sitting in the alley. A shower of glass cut him in a dozen places, but he managed to scramble on to his hands and knees. He was bleeding and dazed, but rapidly scooted away for the sake of his life.

Razer let him go, hurrying to help Lyla with Keene. The two of them got him back into bed. He didn't look in very good shape, but he battled back to become about half-conscious.

'It's OK, Keene,' Razer assured him. 'Everything is OK.'

Keene continued to fight for recovery of his senses. Feeling the bed under him once more, his first concern was to seek out Lyla. When he discovered the girl at his side, he relaxed somewhat.

'You're tougher than buzzard-meat, Keene,' Razer told him. 'Leave you alone for five minutes and you go and pick a fight!'

Lyla was gently dabbing at a cut on his face with a damp cloth. She had a trickle of blood showing at the edge of her own mouth, but her concern was only for him. He forced a weary, consoling smile at them both.

'I'm all right.' With a grimace from taking a breath, 'Guess I'm not up to exchanging punches with anyone just yet.'

'Better get Ragsdale anyway, miss,' Razer told Lyla. 'We better have him take a look at Keene.'

Lyla rushed off to fetch the doctor. It allowed Razer a chance to be alone with Keene for a moment.

'How about that Clemons?' Razer grunted his disgust. 'Dirty old sot came back looking to reclaim his property. I can imagine the kind of plans he had for her.'

'Glad you got here when you did,' Keene told him.

'It was obvious you weren't going to be the hero this time.' Razer emitted a chuckle. 'Someone once said "love conquers all", but I reckon the quotation didn't allow for being shot and about an inch from death at the time. I'm impressed you even managed to get on to your feet.'

'You took good care of Clemons,' Keene replied. 'I didn't see much of the fight, but I caught sight of him going through the window. Hope he broke his neck!'

'No such luck, Keene. They have enough trash

stacked in the alley to break the fall of an elephant. He ran off like a scalded cat.'

'You're pretty good with your fists.'

'I've been in a fight or two, Keene,' he replied.

'I must be getting old. One little hole in my chest and I can't even whip a drunken bum like Clemons.'

'Yep.' Razer grinned. 'You're getting along in years, Keene. Maybe you ought to take up a line of work that is a little less taxing.'

'If I did, who would find the raiders?'

'I'm working on that end of things.' Razer lifted his chin importantly. 'I swore in a new deputy to search the hills and speak to the miners. He's not the kind of man to get run off by a couple hot-head miners.'

Keene frowned. 'You hired another deputy?'

'That right. The man volunteered his help, so I deputized him. I don't know if the city council will want to kick in another forty dollars a month, but we need the help.'

'Who did you get?' Keene wanted to know. 'What man, in his right mind, would be dumb enough to go out into the hills alone and search for the Shadow Killers?'

'He's one of the miners,' Razer explained.

'Which miner?' Keene asked again.

'You've seen him around,' Razer seemed evasive. 'He's a tough number who comes into town on occasion. I think he'll make us a good deputy.'

'But who is he?' Keene raised his voice an octave and glared in exasperation. 'Tell me, Razer! Who'd you hire on as a deputy?'

Razer finally gave in with a short sigh. 'Bull McSwan.'

'What?' Keene's voice squeaked from the high pitch. 'You hired that big bully to work as our deputy?'

'He's seen the error of his ways, Keene. He wants to make amends.'

'Oh, he'll make amends all right. He'll mend everything in town – after he first breaks it into small pieces!'

'Don't be so contrary.' Razer was defensive. 'The guy ain't scared of nothing – unless you count having a snake in his drawers. And I can't be out checking the miners, while you're laid up. If those raiders should attack again, one of us has to be ready to try and prevent another killing.'

Keene closed his eyes and shook his head. 'I wonder what Konrad would say? It's kind of like hiring the James boys to find out who's behind the string of hold-ups on the railroad.'

'Well, if you don't want him working for us, I'll send him over and you can tell him to his face. I'm sure he'll take whatever derogatory remarks you make about his character in stride. He might even not kill you.'

'I wouldn't take odds on that.'

'Say the word and I'll fetch him back.'

Keene rolled his head from side to side. 'Forget it, Razer. Silly me, I let the fact the man is the biggest bully in the country get the best of my judgement. Bull McSwan will probably make us a fine deputy. As I ponder on it, he might be the perfect man to replace Sheriff Cowans.'

Footsteps sounded in the hallway and Razer said: 'Lyla is back with the doctor. I'll check around and see what happened to Clemons. I'll make sure he's left town.'

Ragsdale and Lyla entered, passing Razer as he left the room. Keene let the doctor look over his wound, but he was feeling better already. Cecil had come close with a punch or two, but he hadn't scored a direct hit on his wound. The other little bruises didn't add up to much discomfort.

'I might not be a properly trained physician, but I've a good mind to strap you to your bed, Keene.' Ragsdale's words were austere, but he was smiling. 'Can I trust you not to leave the room for another day or two, or should I get some rope?'

'I'm actually feeling a little tired,' Keene replied. 'I think I'll try and get some rest.'

Ragsdale nodded. 'You were darn lucky the wound wasn't reopened. You best give it a little more time to heal, *before* you start any more brawls.'

'I hear you, Doc.'

Ragsdale flashed a grin. 'I don't get to save many patients, not when they've been wounded as badly as you. Don't ruin my one chance of fame.'

'I'll try not to disappoint you.'

Ragsdale laughed and went out of the room. Lyla closed the door behind him and came back to hover over Keene. She still showed a deep concern for him. He had to smile at that, for her hair was in disarray and the collar of her dress was torn. She'd given no thought to herself.

Reaching up with his right hand, Keene very

tenderly touched a dark blotch on her cheek. Lyla regarded him with her mysterious ebony eyes.

'What is it?' she asked.

'That was a close call with Cecil,' he told her. 'You're going to have to learn to scream – at least shout.'

She lowered her eyes in shame and slowly shook her head. 'I didn't even think about it,' she admitted. 'You were in no shape to save me.'

'I'm afraid you're right on that count.'

A slight curl turned up the corners of her mouth. 'But you did try.'

'Maybe you owe me something for my trouble?' he ventured. 'A kiss maybe?'

'Our last kiss was not one of passion,' she said, 'it was a kiss of compassion.'

Keene frowned. 'Well, maybe we ought to try it again. I don't want you thinking I only feel sorry for you.'

'You seem to be feeling much better,' she teased.

'I'll be fine, Lyla,' he told her. 'You're the one I'm worried about.'

'Me?'

'What is it you want, Lyla? I mean, what do you want out of life?'

She flicked her dark eyes at him and then lowered the lashes once more. The demure act stirred a deep inner emotion within Keene. The little lady seemed to have put her faith and trust in him as blindly as any pup following his master. She had fought like a tiger against Cecil, trying to protect him from harm. She accepted him as her guiding light, the savior who

would shield her from a life of shame and humiliation being married to Cecil. It was an awesome
responsibility.

'You better tell me, Lyla,' Keene whispered softly.
'Or else I'm going to kiss you until you do!'

She blinked in surprise at his threat. 'Keene!' she
pretended indignity. 'Don't you be threatening me.
You can't—'

'Of course.' He cut her argument short. 'I'd have
to have your help. I'm a little too stove-up to reach
out and take you into my arms.'

'You shouldn't be . . .' she appeared flustered. 'I
mean . . . we shouldn't. . . .'

'Come here,' he coaxed, reaching up with his
good hand.

Lyla seemed to hesitate, as if suffering inner
turmoil, before she complied with his request. Boldly
bending down over Keene, she lowered her head
closer to him. Her eyes were veiled by the long-
lashed lids, as she carefully guided her lips down to
touch against his own.

Keene slipped his right hand up behind her head,
applying enough pressure so that he could control
and return the kiss. He was not disappointed, for
after a moment's uncertainty, Lyla was warm and
responsive. The brief encounter was likely the high
point of his entire life, something he would always
cherish.

CHAPTER EIGHT

Tish Bonner set the basket on the small table and offered Keene a charming simper. 'Mrs Fetterman has been telling me to fix you something decent to eat for a week. I was supposed to find you half-dead, unshaven and nearly starved from lack of proper food.' She laughed shortly. 'Instead, you are being spoiled to death by your young lady-friend.'

As she had indicated Lyla, Keene nodded towards her.

'I don't recall if you were properly introduced the night I brought her back to the hotel from the saloon. Her name is Lyla and you're right, she's been babying me ever since I was put to bed. Lyla, you remember Tish Bonner, Todd's lady-friend?'

Lyla gave a nod. 'Nice to see you again, Miss Bonner.'

'You too, Lyla,' Tish replied. 'You look quite tired. Are you trying to work every day and overlook Mr Keene too?'

Lyla shrugged her shoulders, and Tish returned her attention to Keene.

'Todd hired himself a guard. Did he tell you?' she asked him.

'J.T. Reynolds,' Keene replied. 'I don't know much about him, but he sounds capable.'

'It certainly puts a damper on our courtship,' she said with a charming trace of mirth. 'Seems that man is always watching over Todd – even when he isn't needed!'

'From where do you hail, Miss Bonner?'

'Colorado. My mother raised me until she grew sick a couple years back. I went to work and supported her until her death last winter. I was seeking a job, when I learned of an opening for a teacher in Buckshot. The widow, Mrs Fetterman, took me under her wing upon my arrival and put me up at her place. She watches over me like a second mother.' She sighed deeply. 'Trouble is, I wonder if we'll have any children left to teach. Several people have moved out of the valley since the raids started.'

'It might be none of my business, but have you and Todd made any plans for the future?'

She flashed a coy smile. 'Not to the point of setting a date for any special event. We both feel it would be better to keep a certain reserve until this Shadow Killer business is solved.'

'We've narrowed that down some.' Keene tried to lift her spirits. 'As soon as I can get around, I intend to put an end to this raider trouble.'

'Sounds encouraging,' she said enthusiastically. 'Have you told Todd as much?'

'No need getting anyone's hopes up until I'm sure of my facts.'

123

'How much longer before you be able to get around?'

'A few more days yet. I can do a little walking right now, but I don't have much strength or wind.'

Tish glanced at Lyla. 'Well, at least we can be certain you're being watched over. I won't lose any sleep worrying that you aren't eating right.'

'I thank you for the consideration and generous gesture.'

Tish stepped back, her hands clasped in front of her. 'I must get back. Todd expects me to have supper with him and his mother. She is quite concerned for him. What with her husband dying a couple years back and her other son killed by the raiders, Todd is all she has left.'

'Just the four of you, huh?'

Her brows knitted in a lack of understanding. 'Four?'

'You three and the watchdog, Reynolds.'

She laughed at once. 'Just when I was trying to forget about our lack of privacy, you bring him up.'

'Do you know much about him?'

She lifted a careless shoulder. 'No more than most. He used to work at the Little Star mine. I guess he has put that job aside until the Shadow Killers are either caught or they run out of victims and leave of their own accord.'

'Thanks again for the basket of food. I'm flattered you took the time and trouble on my account.'

'Nonsense, Mr Keene. I would have done it for anyone.' She smiled again. 'Besides, Mrs Fetterman wouldn't have been satisfied until I brought something for you. She's one of those types who can't stand the thought of anyone going hungry.'

'I know the type,' Keene said. 'Every town needs at least one like her to look after the strays.'

'She does do that. I'm proof that she doesn't necessarily wait to be asked to jump right in and take charge of a person's affairs.'

Lyla opened the door wide for Tish. It was an invitation to depart and terminate the conversation.

'Thank you, Lyla,' Tish spoke with some warmth. 'I'm glad you're here to take such good care of Mr Keene.'

Lyla returned a fixed smile. She held the door until Tish went out, her skirts rustling as she moved. Then she closed the door to her back and moved over to stand in front of Keene.

Keene had to grin at the stern look on the raven-haired girl's face.

'What a charming young lady,' he teased. 'Wasn't it sweet of her to bring me some fresh bread and rolls? Right neighborly, I'd say.'

But Lyla gave her head an angry shake, her face showing a bit more color than usual. The firm line of her mouth showed that she had her hackles up.

'She doesn't need to come and visit you.'

'She was only being polite,' he maintained, arching his brows in total innocence. 'That Todd Billings is one lucky guy, to have a beautiful and sweet girl like Tish. Don't you think?'

Lyla folded her arms and stomped over to the window. She paused to look out, purposely keeping her back towards Keene.

With a smile, he continued to razz her. 'There sure is a wonderful smell coming from the basket. Why don't you come over here and share it with me? I'll bet Tish is a good cook.'

Lyla spun about, snatched the basket up – then dumped in into his lap with a single move! Whirling about, she strode out of the room and slammed the door behind her.

Keene chuckled to himself. Lyla had a short fuse, when it came to other women. It would be a good thing to remember in the future.

Keene was up and around the next day. He moved stiffly from his wound and was also acutely aware of the new bruises Cecil Clemons had given him. He walked slowly, trying not to jar his body. When he stubbed his toe on the walk a jolt of searing pain knifed through him. He stopped and was doubled over for a few seconds, waiting for the agony to subside. After that, he was careful to pick up his feet.

Razer was asleep in the cell, snoring blissfully. He didn't stir when Keene entered the jail or from the noise of him putting on a pot of coffee. When the brew was hot, Keene dropped an empty pan at the side of his bed. The loud bang finally caused him to come awake, sputtering and rubbing the sleep from his eyes.

'Reflexes like a wolf, alert as a hawk.' Keene laughed. 'Good thing the Shadow Killers aren't after you. You've have been drawn and quartered without even waking up.'

Razer put on an indignant mien. 'It just so

happens I'm acutely attuned to the sounds of my enemies, Keene. I don't fear *your* steps.'

'Yeah, right.'

Razer stretched and let out a body-trembling yawn. Then he got up and came into the office. From the scent that came with him, Keene wished he knew a good rain-dance. 'I know that smelling like a week-dead buffalo is part of your make-up, but is there an unwritten law against taking an occasional bath?'

'I am one of the forest or desert creatures, Keene. If I smelled like rose-water, I'd be at odds with Nature.'

'You're at odds with my nose right now. How do you stand being around yourself all the time?'

'Did you drag yourself out of bed, and from under your little servant's care, only so you could come over and harass me?'

'I needed some exercise. I've got to get on the mend.'

'No argument there,' Razer grunted. 'I've been doing all the work.'

'Any reply to the telegrams yet?'

'No word so far. It'll probably take another couple days. Got to remember we're working on a case history that's five years old.'

'How about your local investigation? Any suspects?'

Razer poured himself a cup of coffee and took a sip. He moved over to the desk and scanned his list of names.

'It isn't going worth a darn, Keene. There are too many people to keep tabs on. With the mining in the hills, the travel through town and the natural flow of people from here to Santa Fe, I can't keep surveillance on all of them.'

'Then we're no closer than we were a week ago.'

Razer sighed. 'Tyler has only been here a short time and admits to knowing a man who might have worked with Vin Hollis. There's also a freighter named Delk whom no one knows much about and, of course, there's Tish Bonner. Other than those three people, there are miners who come and go and a couple ranches who hire seasonal help every year. It doesn't help to shorten our list of suspects any.'

'Are you working on the backgrounds of Delk and Tyler?'

'Tyler came from over near the Colorado border, while Delk is a wanderer from Wyoming. I can't see any tie-in with either of them.' He looked a bit harder at Keene. 'I guess you probably checked out Tish Bonner on your own. Seems I seen her going to your room with a basket of goodies.'

'She was standing with Todd when Hack was burned alive. That means she isn't riding with the killers.' He thought back. 'Tyler was tending bar at the time, too. The only one not accounted for is Delk.'

'I'll keep an eye on his freighting outfit. He does have a couple of men working for him from time to time.'

'We've four men left from that jury five years ago,' Razer recounted. 'If the killing of that Vin Hollis is the reason for these murders. Billings might have been killed to throw us off the right track.'

'Either that, or Todd is still on their list too.'

'It's a possibility,' Razer admitted.

'The four remaining men are Tom Lane, owner of the general store; Ben Carter, who has the leather and tanning shop, Doc Ragsdale and Fred Smith. I think we can consider all of them to be potential targets.'

Razer thought aloud. 'We know Smith is for certain, because they already tried to kill him once.'

'The raiders haven't shot any bystanders and have actually stayed away from town for their first victims. Even when they had you in the room during the foray with Smith, they didn't kill you. That one guy, Link Casto, came after you later.'

'Meaning what?'

'I think these guys are too careful to make a mistake. I believe Billings was an intended victim from the start. His small ranch house is a mile out of town, he lived alone, so he was an easy target. The raiders wanted him.'

Keene pondered the problem. 'We don't have a motive for Billings, Razer. The two boys are known to have been best pals growing up, and their father left the bank to them equally. Todd is the one who put up the money to hire us. I think killing his brother was an act of vengeance by the Shadow Killers. If so, Todd is on the list to be eliminated. The question is, what could two young boys have had in common with the hanging of a convicted murderer?'

'It is the joker of the hand,' Razer replied. 'It makes no sense, and yet you're right. He was killed like the others.'

129

'Maybe we'll get lucky on one of the wires. All we need is a connection, a name, someone who is linked with Vin Hollis.'

'A description would be fine with me, Keene. We're running around like a couple of blind cats trying to catch a mouse in an open field.'

At that moment, the door to the jail swung open. Lyla stood poised, with the sun at her back. She was as beautifully framed as a painting, but there was a frown of disapproval on her face at seeing Keene up and around. She quickly entered the room and came over to his side.

'You weren't in bed,' she said tightly, 'like you're supposed to be.'

'I was trying to get a little exercise.' He excused his disappearance.

Lyla had a small book in her hand. She held it out for him.

'What's this?' Keene asked.

'Look!' was the only word she spoke. Opening the book to a marked page, she pointed to a line and held it out for him and Razer to see.

Keene took the small notebook and recognized it as the diary Cowans had kept. Mostly, he had made entries of happenings, not a daily journal, but items of interest. Once he'd become sheriff, he'd only listed duties and arrests. Bull McSwan was mentioned several times.

'What's it say?' Razer asked, trying to look over his shoulder.

'It's dated the day before the hanging, in the year of eighteen-seventy. Cowans wrote an entry here about the trial.'

'So?' Razer prodded him again. 'Can you read it, or do you need me to help with the bigger words?'

Keene felt a tingle go through him. He started to read aloud, but he already knew they'd been on the right track. Lyla's find substantiated it.

'We all agreed, we twelve jurors, to find Vin Hollis guilty of murder. He could have stopped the fight, once he had his gun out. Instead, he shot and killed Abe Lowell. Judge Billings sentenced him to hang, and hang he will.'

'Billings!' Razer cried. 'The judge was Todd Billings's father!'

'Of course! and Hack Shawn was a witness,' Keene said aloud. 'That ties everyone to the hanging.'

'But old man Billings died a couple years back,' Razer was reasoning it out. 'The raiders couldn't take revenge on him . . . so they struck at his sons!'

'They were all involved in the death of Vin Hollis.'

'All right!' Razer exclaimed happily. 'Billings was a judge, Hack testified against Hollis, and the others were all members of the jury. We've got our motive!'

Keene drew Lyla close and kissed her lightly on the cheek. She flushed from his action but smiled.

'Good work, my little beauty. You've helped to clear up the last part of the mystery concerning the motive for the attacks.'

Her eyes were bright and shining, but their attention was on the antics of Razer. He was hopping and dancing about the room in a manner which seemed to indicate that he had drank too much fire water. The dance appeared to be a mixture of ceremonies – something between a war dance and trying to stomp on a lively cockroach.

'I don't see any reason for celebration yet, Razer,' Keene attempted to calm him down. 'We haven't any suspects. In fact, we don't have a single lead.'

But Razer only whooped and tossed his head. He waved his arms wildly, as his feet pranced and minced under his stocky body. He would not be denied his commemoration of a major breakthrough in their investigation. It mattered not to him that it hadn't changed their complete bewilderment in not discovering the identity of the raiders themselves.

Lyla furrowed her brow and tipped her head at the Indian.

'I don't know,' Keene replied dryly. 'He's rather high-strung for a Shoshone.'

They left Razer dancing and singing in the jail, and Keene tried to recall if the Shoshone even had any kind of war dance.

CHAPTER NINE

Isaac Hayden pinned Cecil Clemons against the tree, a knife pressed up against his throat. Clemons was red-faced from being slapped several times. He rolled his eyes and shook his head back and forth violently.

'Take it easy, Hayden!' he cried, lifting his hands as if he was in the middle of a hold-up. 'I came looking for you. I'm on your side!'

'I'm fer thinking that you're the one what caused all my grief. You done got one of my boys kilt!'

'You kill me and you'll never know what happened to Zeke!' Cecil wailed. 'Listen to me, Hayden!'

Seth stood behind his father wordlessly. Hearing the oath, he put a restraining hand on Isaac's shoulder. The old man glared at Cecil with murderous eyes, but he slowly withdrew the knife from his throat.

'Start talking or you die right now, Clemons!' he ordered harshly. 'What do you know about my boy, Zeke?'

Cecil rubbed a hand along his throat. He drew in

several gulps of air and then explained how Keene and an Indian tracker had hunted down and killed Zeke.

'They claimed it was self-defense, but who's to say what really happened?' he finished the story. 'It's likely Keene discovered Zeke was following along on his back trail and then ambushed and killed him in cold blood. They buried him in the hills, so no one even knows if the bullet is in his chest or his back!'

Isaac lowered his head in sorrow. 'Zeke. . .my boy.' His voice was thick with reverence and grief. 'Half of my family is gone, all on account of that no-good, murderer, Keene!'

'That's why I came to fetch you, Mr Hayden,' Cecil said, hurrying to take advantage of the man's hatred. 'I know how to get to Keene. We can take him before he recovers fully from being wounded.'

'Wounded, you say?' Isaac was all ears. 'How'd that come tuh be? Did Zeke get off a shot hisself?'

'It wasn't Zeke,' Cecil replied. 'It was a gunfight with some stranger in town. Story is, the two of them shot it out on the main street of Buckshot. Keene is still pretty lame from a bullet he took in the chest.'

The old buffalo hunter squinted hard at Cecil. 'And what fer do you want Keene kilt? You done lit out quick enough with him that first night. What changed your mind?'

'He took my wife away from me, Isaac!' Cecil declared. 'I made a trade to marry the little runt and Keene took her for his own! I want her back!'

'We've a debt to settle with her too,' old man Hayden said meaningfully. 'She done started this whole thing.'

'If not for Keene,' Cecil explained to the two of them hastily, 'we could have settled the matter that first afternoon. You could have given her a good beating for beaning your son with a frying-pan and everything would have worked out fine. It's Keene who brung all the trouble for us both. He killed your boy, took away my servant girl, and now he's killed Zeke too!'

Cecil didn't miss Isaac and his remaining son exchanging a knowing look. However, Isaac gave a nod of agreement.

'We'll see to Keene first, Clemons. If'n you play this straight, we might forget the part that your wife played in Joab's death.'

'I'm here to help!' Cecil stated firmly. 'I want to be rid of Keene as badly as you do. It's the reason I came to find you. We need to join forces to beat him!'

With an upward glance at the dark sky, Isaac nodded toward the fire and blankets. 'It's a mite too late to start out tonight. We'll pick up supplies tomorrow and then hit the trail fer Buckshot.'

'Fine, fine.' Cecil spoke with confidence. 'We'll show Keene that he can't mess with us and live to brag about it.'

But even as he moved over to make a bed next to the fire, he spied Isaac speaking in low tones to his son. He couldn't catch the words, but he didn't miss the way Seth flicked a disdainful look in his direction. The slight curl of his lips was enough to make Cecil vow to grab Lyla at the first opportunity and get out of Buckshot. He'd leave the killing of Keene to the Haydens. They were crazy and dangerous. He'd use them to get the runt back, but that was all he needed from them. He didn't trust the filthy hunters one bit. Once they'd served their purpose, he'd be gone like a puff of smoke in a high wind.

Keene was performing the excruciating chore of putting on his boots, when Razer and Bull came bursting into his room. He straightened up and looked at the two implausible lawmen. It was obvious from the excitement in the men's expressions that they were on to something big.

'We've got them!' Bull stated emphatically. 'I done found their hideout back in the hills.'

Keene was all business. 'You've located the raiders? How do you know it's them?'

'I found one of their black masks in their gear. The hood had an opening for eyes in it. It's them all right. Two of them, holed up at the Little Star mine. That place was a dry hole from the start and it ain't been worked in months.'

'It's got to be them,' Razer declared. 'Can't be any other reason for having a black hood in their belongings and camping out at an abandoned mine.'

Bull was anxious. 'What now, Keene? Do we gather a posse?'

Keene gingerly lowered his left arm to his side and hitched his gun belt awkwardly about his waist. He knew he wasn't going to be able to make a long ride out to any mine.

'Round up the men on the jury and Rich Tyler. Have them pick any other men they trust completely. I doubt anyone is going to willingly volunteer to ride

136

with either of you, so let them recruit the help.'

'Thanks for the vote of confidence.' Bull grunted. 'If I was to tell a man to join my posse, he'd darn well join!'

'Yeah, under duress.'

Bull looked blankly at Keene. 'Why would he go underdressed? I ain't going to ask a man to tackle a bunch of killers whilst wearing his long-handles!'

Razer jabbed Bull in the ribs with an elbow. 'Let's get a move on! We need to round up a posse.'

'All right, but they can keep their clothes on. Don't make sense to me to go round underdressed.'

The two men left the room at once. Keene used his right hand to remove and check the loads of his gun. It was from habit, not due to a practical concern for any up-coming action. After all, he couldn't very well join the posse and ride along in a carriage. He would have to let his deputies do the work.

Lyla arrived at the door before Keene could make good his escape to the jail. He didn't have time for idle chatter or explanations, but she still blocked his path.

'What is it, Lyla?' he finally asked. 'I have to get to the office. We've found the Shadow Killers' hideout.'

'Look,' was the only word she said. He gazed down at the page and noticed she had underlined a passage. It listed names of the relatives of the man who was hanged. The wife of Vin Hollis was Ida Reynolds and they had two boys.

'The man guarding Todd Billings is J T Reynolds,' Lyla told Keene. 'He could be using his mother's maiden name.'

137

Keene frowned. 'You're right!' he exclaimed. 'I remember the name now. I saw it before, but it didn't register. Reynolds is the inside man!'

Lyla was nodding her head affirmatively. He patted her on the arm and kissed her quickly. She smiled in response.

'You're not only beautiful, you're smart too,' Keene told her. 'I'll bet that smug character has been laughing himself silly over our stupidity. He's been right under our noses calling the shots. I was going to do some checking on him the day Link Casto took me on in a gunfight. I let his name slip my mind after that.' Keene pictured the man in his mind, cool as ice, even confronting Keene about stealing his horse from the hitching post after Hack Shawn's death. 'It's incredible he had the gall to use his mother's last name all this time. The man obviously possesses nerves of steel.'

'And he's dangerous, Dorret.'

'You stay here at the hotel, Lyla. I've got to get together with a posse and send them out to the Little Star mine. This bit of news only confirms what Bull discovered out in the hills. The place where the Shadow Killers have been hiding also happens to be the mine where Reynolds claimed to have been working!'

She moved aside and Keene hurried out of the room. He didn't exactly run, moving along with the clumsy, breakneck speed of a snail going over a slippery rock. The pain of each step reminded him to keep a slow pace. By the time he reached the bank, his energy was completely spent.

'This a social call?' Todd asked, coming out of his office.

'Any idea where your private guard is at?' Keene panted between breaths.

'He usually comes around about sundown.'

'He might not show tonight.'

'Why not, Keene? What's going on?'

'We've found the Shadow Killers' hideout,' Keene continued. 'I'd like you to join the posse. I can't ride yet, but I've a few men lined up.'

Todd's eyes brightened and his face flooded with excitement. 'You found them!'

'Up at the Little Star mine.'

'The Little Star?' Todd repeated, then groaned. 'Then Reynolds is . . .'

'Yes, he's in with them. No one has worked that mine for a long time. I think Reynolds is the son of Vin Hollis, the man your father sentenced to hang five years ago.'

That brought a new light of understanding into Todd's eyes. 'Then my brother was killed as part of that debt.'

'And you are likely on the list as well. It appears the jury, the judge and even a witness or two were the targets.'

'Maybe he'll show up,' Todd said quickly. 'If he doesn't know about anyone finding the hideout, he might still come to work.'

'Unless he's at the mine with the others,' Keene replied. 'I can't ride yet, so if he should show up here, I'll be waiting to greet him.'

'All right. Who is in charge of the posse?'

139

'Razer is my deputy. He and Bull McSwan will lead the men out to the raider hideout. They are both capable.'

Todd raised his eyebrows. 'Bull McSwan? I thought he was the town bully.'

'Times and people change.' Keene quickly shied away from the subject. 'Meet the others over at the jail in fifteen minutes. Bring your gun and horse.'

'I'll be there.'

Keene remained out of sight during the day. He moved into a position to watch the Billings house and bank. An hour before dark the man appeared. Unaware of Keene, he walked up to the back door and knocked.

'No one home tonight, Reynolds,' Keene said, pointing his gun at the man. 'Billings is out with a posse. I expect they've got your pals by now.'

The young man glowered at Keene. 'So you figured it out, huh?' He grunted his disgust. 'Took long enough.'

'Smith told me about the trial. He said your pa had the other man under his gun. There was no need to kill him.'

'He was cheating,' Reynolds replied. 'He got what he deserved.'

'The gambler was a cheat, but he was unarmed. Had your father given him a beating or chased him out of town, no one would have objected.'

'They lied about him not having a gun!' Reynolds shouted. 'The gambler was one of their own. These miserable sons up and murdered my pa for defending himself!'

'Some of the men you killed were upstanding, moral citizens, Reynolds. I don't believe they are the kind to hang a man without just cause.'

'You're no better than any of them!' he cried. 'You're going to pay too!'

The young man had no chance. Keene already had his gun out and aimed at his chest. It was suicide to draw his weapon . . . but draw he did.

Keene was too unsteady to try and wound the leader of the Shadow Killers. As the man's gun cleared leather, he was forced to pull the trigger.

Reynolds was knocked over by the impact. He landed hard on his back and lay still. Keene swallowed his regret and walked over to look down at the body. The man's eyes were open, but he could no longer see. His hate had consumed him right unto his dying breath.

Lyla was about done with her work for the day. As soon as she removed the heavy sheets from the clothesline behind the hotel her chores were finished. She paused to pull back an unruly lock of hair which dangled into her eyes, tucking it neatly under her scarf. She arched her back, putting her hands on her slight hips. The laborious work and constant bending caused an ache between her shoulders.

She enjoyed a warm sensation at the memory of Keene's loving words and their last embrace. He'd kissed her and held her in his arms. She knew he wasn't the type of man to cheapen a woman. He wouldn't toy with her emotions or take advantage of

141

her. He had said he loved her and she believed it with all of her heart. Marriage had not been spoken of, but she knew he was an honorable man. Once the divorce was final, they would be united.

Even with worry for his safety paramount, she couldn't control the happy, glowing feeling which bathed her like a summer sun. She'd not known love for a long time. Her folks had been hard-working people, but the land was hard and the hot summer and a horde of locusts had destroyed their crops. They might all have starved, had not Cecil come along and offered to buy her for his wife.

She remembered the guilt in her father's eyes, the way he could not even say goodbye to her. He had done what he had to in order to save his family, but he would never be the proud man she had known all of her life. He had sold his daughter into slavery. It would haunt him until the day he died.

Being sold into marriage was upsetting, but to be given to a man like Cecil was more than she could bear. Her mind turned to the episode at the saloon. How utterly degrading, to be stood up in front of a bunch of leering men and have each article of clothing sold right off her back. The humiliation still caused her cheeks to burn with shame. If not for Keene's intervention, when would Cecil have stopped the auction? When she was totally naked!

She shook away the horrid memory. The days of shame and terror were over. Keene would never let any harm come to her again. She put her faith and complete trust in him. He was a part of a new life for her, one they would share together.

Suddenly, her serene thoughts were shattered. A meaty hand clamped over her mouth and she was jolted back to a harsh reality!

Lyla struggled, but a powerful arm was wrapped around her, pinning her arms. She was dragged from the back yard of the hotel and into the nearby brush. She struck out at the assailant, trying to claw at the man who held her. She could smell dried blood and a foul odor – the same that she had known once before. When she squirmed around enough to see, she located her attacker. It was one of the buffalo hunters!

'Quit your fighting, you little she-devil!' Seth Hayden snarled. His hand left her mouth and he tore off her scarf. Then, jerking her around to face him, his fist smacked her hard in the jaw. The punch knocked her backward and she landed flat on her back!

Lyla was stunned, but threw up her hands to protect her face, fearful he was going to hit her again. But Seth was concerned about getting out of Buckshot quietly. He didn't want any prolonged battle. He forced her to bite down on the scarf and tied it about her head. Then his dirty paw grabbed a handful of her hair and he lifted her back to her feet.

'Your husband, Clemons, is waiting fer us.' He grinned with malevolent eyes. 'If you want to live to see another day, you won't give me any call to knock you down a second time.'

Lyla's head was tipped back from the man's mangy fist being entangled in her hair. He pulled her over backwards until she had to rely on his other hand to support her and keep her from falling. She was breathing hard, and it caused him to regard the rise and fall of her breasts with an unwanted amount of attention.

'What do you say?' he asked. 'You going to co-operate?'

Lyla nodded affirmatively. It seemed to cause Seth a slight measure of disappointment. She had the feeling he would have enjoyed roughing her up some more.

Seth tossed a piece of paper into her laundry basket, released his hold of her hair and violently shoved her forward. Before she could get her balance, he took hold of her arm. His cruel fingers taloned into the soft flesh above her elbow. She did her best to keep pace with him as he dragged and pushed her along a back-street and out of town.

Lyla looked for help, but there wasn't anyone in sight. When the two of them left the buildings for the nearby hills, she knew her fate was sealed. Keene wouldn't know what had happened to her. He might even assume that she'd been taken by the Shadow Killers.

Once into the trees, Seth led her up a narrow path. She was shocked to see Isaac and Cecil Clemons together. Of all the low-down, subhuman acts she might have thought Cecil capable of, joining forces with the Haydens was right at the bottom of the list.

'I've missed you, runt,' Cecil said, displaying a sickening smirk on his ugly face. 'I can't tell you how much harder it is to earn a living without you to help out.'

'And I'm lookin' forward to having your guardian come to get you back,' Isaac sneered through his yellow, rotted teeth. 'He done kilt two of my boys. I aim to see he pays the price fer that.'

Seth turned her loose and laughed. 'I say we kill him real slow, Pa. I want to see him squirm and beg.'

Isaac looked off in the direction of Buckshot. 'We want him on our own terms, son. Did you leave the note?'

'Right thar in her work-basket, Pa. Keene is sure to come hunting us, soon as he finds it.'

Isaac was satisfied with the answer and looked over at Cecil. 'If that wife of yourn makes a break fer the tall timber, it'll be your neck, Clemons. You best keep that thought in mind.'

Cecil hurried over to take hold of Lyla's wrist. He jerked her over to stand close to him. 'Not to worry,' he put on a pasty grin. 'The runt won't cause no trouble. I promise you that.'

Isaac ran vulgar eyes over Lyla, lingering on her feminine attributes. One corner of his mouth turned upwards in a sinister smirk.

'Mayhaps we'll find a way of entertaining the she-cat, Clemons. Once Keene is dead, she might be in need of some comfort.'

Cecil shook his head. 'You promised that I could take the runt and leave, once you had Keene.'

Isaac flicked him a dull, unconcerned look. 'Sure, sure, I 'member what I done told you. Let's get moving.'

'How long do you think, Pa?' Seth asked.

'He'll be along, son,' Isaac said firmly. 'We've

plenty of time. We'll just sit back and wait fer Keene to show.'

'Think he'll do as you told him in the note and come alone?'

'If'n he has any concern fer the gal, he will,' Isaac sneered. Then, molesting Lyla with his eyes, 'I figure he'll do exactly as we told him.'

Lyla was forced up onto a horse. Cecil was taking no chances. He tied her hands and took the reins of her mount. She glared at him with hot, smoldering eyes, wishing she could tell him what a piece of low-life vermin he was.

The four of them started off, directing the horses up through the trees toward the main trail. Lyla had no idea where they were taking her, but she knew the reason for the abduction was to draw Keene into a fight. He had not yet recovered from the wound he had received from Link Casto. Now he would have to face both Isaac and his son. The odds were not good.

But Lyla knew something of Keene's determination. She had no doubt he would come. He would follow the orders on the note, which probably warned him that she would be killed should he bring help. He wouldn't risk her life, so he would come to face Seth and Isaac alone. If not for hoping against all odds that he could somehow rescue her, she might have attempted to end her own life. The few precious moments when he'd held her close, the sweetness in his voice, as he told her that he cared for her – that would be worth dying for.

However, Lyla was also a survivor. If Keene was killed, she would do whatever it took to see that Seth and Isaac were also put to death. She would find a way to get word to the US marshal, or she would manage to contact Razer. Even if it meant cutting their throats as they slept, she would make certain his death was avenged.

She attempted to drive the negative thoughts from her head. Keene wasn't dead yet, and she was not helpless. It didn't escape her attention, the way Seth kept looking at the exposed part of her legs. The dress she wore was not meant for riding. The material rode up above her knees, showing evidence of the shapeliness of her legs. The man's eyes were like dirty hands, exploring the bare flesh. She dared not think what he had in mind for her.

Instead, she kept her thoughts on how to escape. Being bound in the saddle and surrounded by Cecil and the two hunters, she had no chance to bolt for freedom. However, they would relax the vigil once they made camp. If the opportunity came for getting away, she would grab it at once. Her every waking moment had to be spent trying to devise a manner of escape. She had to somehow keep these vile, barbarous men from drawing Keene into their trap and killing him.

CHAPTER TEN

The fire was burning brightly, bathing the clearing in a luminous glow, which reflected off the surrounding trees and brush. A post had been set a few feet from where the logs crackled and were being consumed by the flames. Lyla was bound to the post like a witch being readied to burn at the stake.

Cecil fed the camp-fire and appeared to be awaiting Keene's arrival. To entice Keene into being careless, Lyla's pale blue blouse was torn open to reveal the white camisole beneath. Her face was either bruised or dirty, giving the appearance that she had been physically abused.

Keene ventured close enough to survey the camp. He could see two horses on a picket line, plus Cecil and Lyla. But there had been prints of at least four horses on the trail. The smell of a trap permeated the air and assailed his senses. Cecil wouldn't have the intestinal fortitude to devise such an invitation on his own. Nor was he the brave sort to offer himself as live bait. That meant the planning was not old man Clemons's. As sure as the girl was tied out in the open, there was at least one bushwhacker sitting back in the dark.

Keene held his rifle in one hand, moving with cunning and stealth, careful not to disturb branches or crush sticks or leaves underfoot. Going down onto his hands and knees, he eased to the edge of the camp's light. He had a clear shot at Cecil, but that didn't matter. The miserable sot wasn't his first concern.

'We know you be out there, Keene!' A horribly familiar voice rang out loud and clear. 'You come on into the light afore we put a torch to your gal!'

Keene stayed where he was. Isaac could have been guessing. They might not know he was in the area at all. He slipped his rifle forward and swept the circle of trees and brush. The voice had come from the opposite side of the camp.

'Mayhaps you don't think I mean business, Keene. Is that it?'

Moving his finger past the trigger guard, Keene eased the rifle into firing position. He watched for the slightest movement. He had to assume Seth was also out in the dark, poised and ready to kill.

'No use playing possum with us, Keene. We done rounded up your horse a half-hour ago. You coming out? Or do we get serious about this here game of cat and mouse?'

Keene cursed his clumsy approach. If he hadn't been so drained of strength, he would have stopped a full mile short of the camp and skirted around enough to come in from the far side. If he were healthy, he might have gotten in undetected. He searched for an idea, but he couldn't bluff them with silence. They knew he was watching the clearing. Once they got rough with Lyla, he would be forced to give himself up. That would mean his death and cast her fate into the hands of the scumbag buffalo-hunters and Clemons – not a pleasant scenario.

Seth Hayden appeared out of the trees. Isaac risked having him step out in the open, while he sat back and waited for a clear shot. Seth led Keene's horse over to one side of the camp and tied the animal to a tree branch. He looked around then, slowly gazing past Keene's position. They knew he was out there, but had not yet discovered his exact location.

As quietly and carefully as he could, Keene edged away from the fire's light. He began painstakingly to pick his way through the brush, beginning a circle around the clearing. If he could locate Isaac and take him out, he would be able to deal with Seth on even terms.

However, Isaac knew better than to sit patiently and let Keene maneuver his way through the dark until he located him.

'Best show Keene that we mean business, son,' the old man's voice boomed, still too far away to pick out in the dark. 'Keep your eyes on this, you murdering tin star!'

Seth had fashioned himself a torch. He doused the rag-wrapped end with something which appeared to be lantern-oil. Then he took the pail of fuel over to where Lyla was bound. As Keene felt his heart stop, the buffalo hunter splashed the liquid on to her dress and blouse.

'You watching, Keene?' Isaac's voice was full of malice and a smug confidence. He knew victory was within his grasp. 'You going to sit back and see your gal go up in flames like Seth's torch?'

Seth put his fashioned stick into the fire. Fire nearly exploded from the rags. Then the young Hayden held it out in the direction of Lyla, menacing her, holding it a foot or so from her eyes! It would take but a spark, a drop of burning rag to ignite her clothes!

An unholy terror flooded Lyla's face. She strained at the ropes that bound her with all of her might, twisting violently. She jerked against her bonds and threw her head back and forth.

'Looks like your little friend don't like the idea of being set on fire, Keene.' Isaac sneered at her strenuous reaction. 'You want fer us to roast her alive?'

'Shall I show him now, Pa?' Seth cried gleefully. 'Is it time fer a demonstration?'

Isaac laughed wickedly. 'Do it, son.'

Keene had no idea what was going on. He found a clear field of fire and aimed his rifle at Seth. If he moved one inch closer to Lyla he'd kill him. Even if Isaac was to shoot and kill her in return, he would not let her be burned alive.

However, Seth didn't make a move in that direction. He rotated about and sloshed the remainder of the fuel oil on Cecil! The man sputtered with surprise.

'What the devil are you doing?' he cried out, wiping the liquid from his face and eyes. 'Get away from me!'

But before he could retreat, Seth reached out and

151

touched him with the fiery end of the torch!

Cecil shrieked in terror, an ear-piercing cry which shattered the night, echoing off of the walls of the nearby mountains. Lyla screamed at the sight as well, her own shriek of horror blending with the wailing cries of Cecil, as he was being burned alive by the voracious flames.

Keene was stunned for a moment, unable to react at once. Cecil was a walking bonfire from head to foot, flailing with his arms, staggering blindly. There was no chance to douse the fire or beat it out. In his stumbling, he turned toward Lyla. If he got too close, if his burning flesh contacted her oil-soaked clothing. . . !

Keene threw his rifle to his shoulder and ended Cecil's misery with a bullet to the heart. The shot knocked him away from Lyla. His body sprawled in death, as the fire continued to burn.

Seth saw the direction from where his shot had come. He quickly moved behind Lyla, using her as cover. He still held the torch, stuck out well behind him, lest he set fire to the girl accidentally. Keene had no clear shot at him.

'She's next!' Isaac bellowed. 'Come on out, Keene. Show yourself or she burns next!'

Keene glanced at Cecil's remains. His corpse had become a smoldering lump of charred flesh. Seeing the faceless mass roll with a final reflexive twitch, Keene turned his eyes away.

'Ten seconds, Keene!' Isaac bellowed at the top of his lungs. 'Come out or your gal is going to become a barbecue!'

It meant certain death, but Keene couldn't sit back

and let Lyla be burned alive. Even if he got off a lucky shot and hit Seth, there was a possibility the man would torch Lyla's clothing as he went down. He couldn't take that chance. With a sigh of defeat, Keene pushed through the brush and walked into the firelight.

'Drop your guns right there!' Isaac shouted from the darkness. 'I want to see them fall.'

Keene did as instructed. He tossed the rifle a few feet away, then unhitched his gun belt and let it drop as well. Seth tossed his torch into the fire and pulled his handgun. Lyla had managed to gather her composure, but was still visibly trembling over watching Cecil be burned alive. She focused her eyes on Keene, as he entered into the flickering light of the fire. He could see the regret and sorrow in her make-up. This was to be their farewell.

'We got him, Pa,' Seth yelled gleefully. 'He's ours!'

Keene lifted his hands up even with his shoulders and looked at Lyla. There were so many things he wanted to say to her, so many things. . . .

'I'm sorry!' she sobbed. 'I'm so sorry, Dorret.'

He stared back at her, wishing he had some way to save her. Once he was dead, the Haydens could do whatever they wanted to her. He cursed his failure. Maybe he should have taken his shot – tried to take out Seth and hope old man Hayden returned fire at him. It was likely he had missed his one and only chance.

Seth didn't give him and Lyla time for any reunion. He pulled his pistol and pointed it at Keene. He moved closer, stepping over the still-smoking body of Cecil Clemons. Keene suffered a monumental regret. What a dirty shame that he was going to die. He'd so have enjoyed spending his life with Lyla.

Isaac entered into the firelight, showing himself, confident he had Keene where he wanted him. The man's big buffalo gun was pointed at Keene. A cruel sneer displayed his tobacco-stained teeth, as he guffawed loudly.

'Look at him, son. Look at the big killer-man. He don't look so tough no more.'

'Let me show him what fer, Pa,' Seth pleaded, his eyes dancing with fire. 'Let me even the score for Joab and Zeke.'

'Time enough to do this thing right, son. We'll make sure he suffers a long and agonizing death.' He set a frosty gaze on Keene. 'Just the way I've had to suffer the loss of my boys.'

'You're the same as your weasel sons,' Keene taunted him. 'None of you has the guts to fight like men. That's probably why you're buffalo hunters. You kill your prey from a long way off, so there's no chance of them fighting back. You cowardly Haydens are nothing more than a family of lily-livered cadavers.'

'Mouthy sort, ain't he?' Seth laughed. Then he put a curious gaze on Isaac. 'What fer be a cadaver, Pa?'

Isaac shrugged his shoulders. 'Mayhaps a varmint of some kind.'

'Varmint, huh?' And Seth swung his rifle at Keene.

Keene ducked away, but he was unable to avoid being struck a glancing blow with the barrel of the man's gun. It grazed Keene's cheek and caught him off the top of his shoulder. It wasn't square enough to knock him down, but it staggered him backwards a step.

'Stop it!' Lyla cried. 'You're the ones who started

the fight! We never did anything to you! The death of both of your sons is due to your trying to kill Dorret! You're the ones who brought about the death of your own boys!'

'I done liked her better afore she went to runnin' off at the mouth,' Seth told his old man. 'What we going to do about her?'

'She opens her yap again, you give Keene another wallop with your gun. Every time she makes a peep, you bust Keene.' He showed a sneer. 'You probably heared the saying how a woman can talk a man to death. Well, this here be the case in point.'

Keene feigned being hurt worse than he was, rubbing his cheek and showing unsteady legs. If he could get close enough to Seth, he might somehow grab him and wrestle away his gun.

But Isaac was taking no chances. He drew a bead on Keene with his big .50 caliber rifle. He shut one eye and sought out a specific target.

'How many times do you think I kin hit Keene and not kill him outright?' he asked his son.

'No more'n twice with your cannon, Pa. That big fifty will blow a hole in him the size of your fist. Two holes that big will kill any man.'

Isaac lowered the long gun. 'All right, son. I'll let you put the first one in him. See if you kin pop a kneecap or elbow. We'll use a bullet to break both his arms and his legs, then we kin sit back and watch him crawl around like a worm, until he begs fer death.'

Seth chuckled. 'I hear you, Pa.' Then he took aim at Keene's right leg. Keene searched frantically for a weapon, a way to fight back. But there was nothing at hand. He was doomed to die. He set his teeth, prepared for the shock of the bullet striking his flesh.

A gunshot rocked the mountain walls.

Keene flinched, expecting to feel the passing of the white-hot slug through part of his body. He knew the violent contact would knock him down, that the incredible pain would force him to cry out.

Except the jolt didn't come.

Seth staggered to one side and pitched onto his face, his gun lost from his grip. He twisted onto his side, his eyes and mouth both open in surprise and shock. Even as Keene realized the gunshot had come from someone other than Seth, a groan of death escaped his lips.

Bull McSwan came charging across the clearing. Isaac swung his big buffalo gun around, but he was too slow. Bull took him down with a brutal tackle. They rolled on the ground and struggled for a moment. Then both scrambled onto their feet with knives drawn and extended.

Bull appeared big and awkward, but he wasn't clumsy. He and Isaac circled one another, while Razer sauntered over to cut the cords which held Lyla. Keene started over to pick up Seth's gun, but Razer stopped him.

'Let them have at it, Keene,' he said. 'The old bear is McSwan's meat. Let him earn his pay.'

Lyla came free of the ropes and rushed into Keene's arms. He held her close and backed away from the fire, where the two men were locked in mortal combat.

Isaac took a vicious swipe with his blade, but Bull spun away, countering with his own knife. They traded jabs and warily circled again.

'I'm gonna gut you, big man,' Isaac sneered. 'I'm gonna spill your innards on the ground and stomp them under my heel!'

Bull backed up a step. He stood up straight and pulled his shirt up to expose his broad, hair-covered chest. 'Here you go, tough guy,' he sneered, 'Let's see if you can carve your name on my belly before I cut your heart out.'

Isaac lunged forward, sweeping his knife back and forth, trying to find flesh with the deadly weapon.

But Bull jumped to the side and took an upward slash with his own knife. The blade caught Isaac under his guard and sliced a six-inch gash down his forearm. It should have slowed the buffalo hunter down, but it only made him more determined.

The two came together, each locking a hand over the other's knife-wielding wrist. They strained with all of their might, pitting strength against strength.

Bull gave ground for a step or two, until he got his balance. Then he took control. He was younger and physically superior to Hayden. With a violent change in direction, he turned Isaac's knife away from himself. In the same motion, he drove his own blade up and into the man's stomach.

Keene heard the sickening squelch of the knife entering a human body. Isaac's eyes bugged from their sockets, as Bull wrenched the blade upward, burying it to the hilt. He lifted the man up onto his toes, as he drove the blade into his heart. Then he stepped back and let the buffalo hunter fall. Isaac was dead before his head bounced off the hard ground.

Lyla buried her face against Keene's shoulder. Bull stood over the body, winded from the deadly battle. Only Razer took the episode in his stride. He walked over and patted the big man on the back.

'You're about as skillful at knife-fighting as an Indian squaw, McSwan, but you did get the job done.'

Bull took a deep breath, his massive chest still heaving from his exertion. 'And I suppose you'd have done it quicker and cleaner?'

'Ten seconds – tops!'

'Let's see if you two are as good with shovels as you are with knives.' Keene broke up the friendly interplay. 'This place is going to look like a graveyard by the time we've planted all the bodies.'

Keene didn't offer to dig any holes. He was feeling weak from the long hours in the saddle. He led Lyla down to the edge of a small stream and wet his bandanna. Then he carefully removed traces of blood from her abraded wrists.

He spoke to break the uneasy strain from the night's experience. 'Took all the hide off, twisting around like that.'

'I smell like lamp-oil,' she replied.

He smiled at her. 'On you, it smells good.'

At last she relaxed. With the camp out of sight, she was able to get her mind off the ghastly deaths. She took a seat on a fallen log and waited until Keene had sat down next to her.

'You might have given me a wink or some kind of sign,' she scolded him. 'I thought the Haydens were going to shoot a dozen holes in you.'

Keene swallowed ignominiously. 'Yeah, well I . . .'

158

he gave her a sheepish look, 'I didn't actually know I had any help. Bull and Razer arrived in town as I was leaving. The posse shot it out and killed the other two Shadow Killers. When I told them you had been kidnapped, they wanted to come along. I told them no, because the note said you would be killed. As far as I knew, they stayed behind in Buckshot.'

'You came alone? To let yourself be captured?' she said in an accusing tone. 'You would have forced me to watch you die, then left me to those two swine!'

'I didn't have a choice.'

'Oh yes you did!' she countered. 'You should have shot Seth and taken your chances with Isaac. What kind of man lets the woman he loves sit back and watch him be tortured and killed?'

'Lyla, I—'

'And then they would have been free to do whatever they wanted to me!' She continued to rant at him. 'What were you thinking!'

'I wasn't thinking,' he admitted lamely. 'I was trying to keep them from killing you.'

'Oh!' she complained bitterly, 'and you didn't think I would have preferred death to watching you be brutally murdered and being left in their hands?'

Keene groaned in defeat. 'Dad-gum, woman! I did what I thought I had to do.'

She finally simmered. 'It's lucky for you that your friends showed up.'

'Yes, it is.'

'Otherwise we'd both have ended up dead! I swear, if that's the way you think under pressure, you're in the wrong line of work.'

'This was only a temporary appointment,' he told her. 'I'm done being a lawman.'

Lyla appeared ready to unleash another barrage of criticism, but Keene didn't give her the chance. He pulled her into his arms and smothered her with a passionate, dominating kiss. He didn't allow her a breath or retreat for a full minute. When he finally broke contact, Lyla was out of breath.

'Let's call a truce about my lack of tactics on this rescue . . . OK?'

A impish smile surfaced along her lips. 'I suppose I can forgive you.'

'I promise not to let you be taken by any blood-thirsty buffalo hunters ever again.'

'All right. I'll try not to put my own life in jeopardy either,' she agreed.

'It's a deal.'

Lyla was not finished. 'And, while I'll always owe Bull and Razer a debt of gratitude, that's as far as it goes.'

'What do you mean?' he asked.

The simper lingered on her lips. 'I don't intend to name our children Bull or Razer. You'll forgive me, but those are not the proper titles I've envisioned for our kids.'

Keene laughed at the thought. 'It might break their hearts, but I'm in complete agreement with you.'

She softly murmured: 'I love you, Dorret.'

Knowing those words made up the most beautiful sentence he could ever hear, Keene did what any moderately intelligent man would do . . . he kissed Lyla again.